P

CAN'T STOP US NOW

C.C., Annette, Robin and Gail can't believe their
luck when they're chosen as the members of a new
all-girl rock band. They're an unlikely mixture from
all over New York but they agree on one thing –
that making music is the most important thing in
their lives. They have the talent and determination
and share the same dream of becoming rock stars.
Their manager, Reg Barthwaite, has all the experience and contacts and so they're sure that it
won't be long before they'll be famous as the
members of *Overnight Sensation*.

But Reg has his own ideas for the band which are
more to do with making money than music. He can
make them stars but only if they play by his rules.
Do they want stardom on Reg's terms? They soon
discover that it will be much harder than they
thought to make their dream come true. There are
some difficult choices to be made on the road to
success – will they choose the right way?

Fran Lantz is a former rock musician, children's
librarian and nanny. She lives in Brookline,
Massachusetts, with her husband, three guitars, and
a large rock 'n' roll record collection.

FRAN LANTZ

CAN'T STOP US NOW

PENGUIN BOOKS

PENGUIN BOOKS

Penguin Books Ltd, 27 Wrights Lane, London W8 5TZ (Publishing and Editorial)
and Harmondsworth, Middlesex, England (Distribution and Warehouse)
Viking Penguin Inc., 40 West 23rd Street, New York, New York 10010, USA
Penguin Books Australia Ltd, Ringwood, Victoria, Australia
Penguin Books Canada Ltd, 2801 John Street, Markham, Ontario, Canada L3R 1B4
Penguin Books (NZ) Ltd, 182–190 Wairau Road, Auckland 10, New Zealand

First published in the USA by Dell Publishing Co., Inc. 1986
Published in Penguin Books 1988

Printed and bound in Great Britain by
Cox & Wyman Ltd, Reading

For John

Overnight Sensation's most loyal fan

Robin Quinn slipped her electric guitar over her shoulder and switched on her amplifier. With a joyous smile she pushed the volume knob as far up as it would go and hit the strings. The result was almost overwhelming—a solid wall of sound that filled her tiny bedroom and bounced off the ceiling and the walls. Quickly she tore into the introduction of her latest song and began to sing.

> *Well, I may be crazy, but I've got this dream,*
> *I'm gonna make the whole world stand up and scream.*
> *I gotta find me a place where I belong,*
> *So don't try to hold me down, cuz I'll be gone, gone, gone.*

That was when the banging started, a continuous thumping that vibrated up through Robin's bare feet. She tried to ignore it by singing even louder. "You can't stop me now!" she wailed. "No, you can't stop me now." When she finished the chorus the banging stopped, only to be replaced by the jangling ring of the telephone.

With a sigh Robin stopped playing, unplugged her guitar, and walked into the kitchen. She didn't have to wonder who was on the phone. Old Mrs. Philbin always thumped her broom on the ceiling when the noise got too loud. Just last week, in fact, she'd warned Robin that if the guitar playing got any louder she'd forego the broom and just call the police.

Robin grabbed the receiver by the wire and dangled it in front of her face. "I'm sorry, Mrs. Philbin," she yelled into the mouthpiece. "Don't call the cops. I'll turn it down." Without waiting for a reply she hung up and walked slowly back to the bedroom, feeling decidedly glum.

"Fat chance *you'll* ever be a rock star," she told the reflection in her bureau mirror. "You haven't even got a place to practice, let alone a band."

Stretching her long body across her bed, she rested her guitar on her stomach and played a lead line she'd memorized from a Stevie Ray Vaughn album. As she picked out the notes, she stared up at the Woodstock poster that hung over her desk. Her parents had gone to the 1969 Woodstock Music Festival and taken three-year-old Robin along with them. From where she lay on the bed, she could just make out her face on the poster— a grinning ragamuffin in a crowd of four hundred thousand hippies.

Robin's memories of the weekend were vague—crowds, rain, mud, snuggling with her mother in a sleeping bag, sharing an apple with her dad. But most of all she remembered the music and the good feeling it had given her. Jimi Hendrix's searing guitar lines, Janis Joplin's wailing voice, the wild rhythms of Santana—she'd loved it all. Looking back, Robin knew she had fallen in love with rock 'n' roll that weekend. In fact, she'd wanted to be a rock musician ever since.

Robin's thoughts were cut short when she heard the front door open. "Mom?" she called, sitting up in the bed. "Hank?"

"Nope," her father answered. "Just dear old Dad."

A moment later he appeared at the bedroom door. His thinning brown hair was ruffled and the collar of his corduroy jacket had been turned up against the autumn wind.

"Hi, Dad. No class this afternoon?" Mr. Quinn was a sociology professor at NYU, and like that of the rest of the family, his schedule changed from day to day.

"Just a meeting with the dean, but I skipped out early. I couldn't take another boring debate over who should chair the soc department next year. It's all politics anyway. That windbag Peterson's a shoe-in."

Robin laughed and pushed her curly brown hair out of her eyes. She liked her father's irreverent attitude. Unlike most adults he had a healthy distrust of authority and a steadfast hatred of hypocrisy. "So," her dad continued, "what's new with you?"

She frowned. "I might as well tell you before you hear it firsthand," she told him. "Mrs. Philbin had her broom out this afternoon."

"Oh, Robin!" Mr. Quinn sighed. "Sometimes I'd like to throw that amp of yours out the window."

Robin shot her father an impish smile. "Bad idea, Dad. Mrs. Philbin always lets her dog out right under my window. You wouldn't want to take a chance on crushing little Fifi, now, would you?"

Mr. Quinn chuckled and shook his head. "Listen, rock star, I'm serious. You know I think your music is great, but if you're going to practice in here, you've got to keep the volume down."

Robin started to protest, then thought better of it. "Yes, sir," she answered with a resigned nod.

"Good." Her father smiled. "Mom's picking up Hank and they'll be home any minute. Come on out and help me start dinner."

Jumping up, Robin turned off her guitar and followed her father into the kitchen. They were peeling potatoes when the phone rang. "It'll be Matt," she said, dropping a half-peeled potato into the sink and running down the hall to the extension in her parents' room.

Robin threw herself across the double bed and grabbed the receiver before the second ring. "Hi!" she gasped. "Matt?"

"None other. Listen, did you decide where you want to go tonight?"

Robin didn't answer right away. Hearing Matt's voice always gave her a little thrill, and she wanted to savor it. She pictured him leaning against the pay phone outside his dorm room. She could see his blue eyes, his straight brown hair, and the cute little mole on his right cheek. Mmm, nice . . .

"Robin, are you there?"

"Oh, yeah, uh, sorry. I was just thinking about tonight. Hey," she exclaimed, "I've got an idea! You can come over and help me work out a harmony for my new song. Then later we can watch *Friday Night Videos.*"

Matt moaned. "Robin, you know I'm tone deaf. Besides, I want to go out tonight."

Robin grabbed the latest copy of *The Village Voice* from the bedside table. "Okay, I'll look at the concert listings."

He laughed. "You've got a one-track mind." More seriously he added, "Robin, we've been going out together for over a month now, and all you ever want to do is go to rock concerts. Don't you ever get sick of hanging around in those smoky little clubs? They're so crowded and noisy."

Robin thought it over. Admittedly, some things about rock clubs—the crowds, the smoke, the high cover charge—were not too appealing. But as far as she was concerned that was a small price to pay to see the bands and hear the music. "I love it," she answered. "Besides, if I want to make it in rock 'n' roll, I have to follow the club scene."

"Jeez," Matt muttered, "you sound like a groupie or something."

Robin's fingers tightened around the receiver. "A groupie! Is that what you think I am?"

"Of course not," he said with a chuckle. "I was only kidding. But you have to admit, you do seem a little obsessed sometimes."

"Well, why shouldn't I be?" Robin asked defensively. "I'm a rock musician. I'll never become famous if I don't take it seriously."

"All right already. I'm not trying to get into a fight. But, don't forget, you're not the only person around here who wants to be famous. I'm a theater major, remember? How am I ever going to learn to be the new Robert Redford if we don't go to the movies once in a while?"

"The movies?" Robin asked dubiously.

"Yeah, you know, they take a series of little pictures and project them onto a screen. It's really quite clever."

Robin giggled. "Okay, okay. I get the point. We'll go to a movie tonight."

"Great. Listen, why don't I come right over? We can look at the film listings when I get there."

"Okay. See ya soon," she answered, hanging up the phone.

Lying back across her parents' bed, Robin stared up at the ceiling and considered what Matt had said. A groupie, huh? she thought with irritation. I've told him at least a dozen times I want to be a rock musician. Why doesn't he take me seriously?

Robin rolled on her stomach and sighed. Then again, she asked herself, why should he? While I talk about being a star, Matt's actually out there becoming one. The semester's only a few weeks old and already he's got the lead in the Drama Department's first play, *Manhattan Magic*. Meanwhile I'm just sitting around my house, getting nowhere. I'm not even in a band.

Robin thought back to her old high school band, Blacktop. They'd had three good years together, playing at school dances and friends' parties, but when graduation rolled around, the band members had gone their separate ways. Robin had been trying to find a new band ever since, but so far nothing had worked out. Either the group was too old, too young, too far away, or they played music Robin couldn't stand. Or they were all stoned out of their minds. Or they couldn't handle the idea of a girl guitarist. The only band that had really seemed like a possibility—a dance band called Green Peas—had broken up after only one rehearsal.

"If I don't get in a band soon," she muttered, "I'm going to scream." With a frown she sat up and opened *The Village Voice*, planning to check out the movie listings before Matt showed up. Flipping through the paper she searched for the film page, but paused when she noticed the "Musicians Wanted" section in the classifieds.

Without really meaning to Robin found herself glancing over the ads. *Heavy metal band seeks ballsy lead singer.* Not quite. Heavy metal wasn't Robin's kind of music, and besides, she was a guitarist, not a lead singer. *Drummer wanted for Top Forty cover group.* 'Fraid not. *Wanted: Teenage musicians for all-girl rock band.*

Robin froze and her heart seemed to skip a beat. Now, *this* sounded like a real possibility. Quickly she read the ad again. *Wanted: Teenage musicians for all-girl rock band. Call 555-2162 and ask for Reg.*

A million questions flashed through Robin's mind. Who was Reg? Why an all-girl band? What kind of music would they play? But before she could come up with any answers, Robin heard the front door open and her brother ask, "What's for dinner?"

"Robin!" her father called. "Mom and Hank are here. Get off the phone and set the table!"

"Coming!" Quickly Robin tore out the ad for the all-girl band and stuffed it into her pocket. First thing after dinner she'd call Reg and find out what he had in mind.

Robin half walked, half danced into the kitchen, her mind filled with images of recording sessions, concert dates, and a hit album with her photo on the cover. Her phone conversation, the movie listings, ever her date tonight, were completely forgotten. This was a chance to join a band, and compared to that, nothing else really mattered.

|||||||||||||||||||||||| *2*

"Maybe I should just wait outside," Gail suggested, backing down the steps that led to the warehouse. "I mean, I don't know anything about rock 'n' roll. . . ."

"No way," Suzi answered firmly. "You promised you'd come along and help me out. You can't back out now. Besides, anybody can play rock. Even a classical egghead like you. All you have to do is play the music I gave you and I guarantee it'll sound great."

Gail didn't answer. While Suzi rang the bell, she thrust her hands into her jacket pockets and looked around. This was the first time she'd ever been in this part of Manhattan—SoHo, it was called. The main streets were lined with art galleries and restaurants, and the clothing store on the corner featured a window display of bald mannequins dressed in leather and chains. Here on Greene Street between Canal and Grand the street was paved with cobblestones and the buildings were mostly dingy textile warehouses. Posters were plastered all over the lampposts advertising rock groups and clubs.

It's weird, Gail thought, how you can live your whole life in New York City and never venture outside your own little neighborhood. When I was growing up in the Bronx, lower Manhattan seemed like another world. But in my new neighborhood in New Jersey, kids like Suzi come into the city every weekend. I guess that's just one of the differences, she reflected, between having money and being poor.

When the door was buzzed open, Suzi and Gail hurried inside. Dirty concrete stairs with a metal railing led up to a series of blank brown doors. "Are you sure this is the right building?" Gail asked.

"Sure I'm sure. Just keep going. See," Suzi said when they reached the top floor. A sign on the door read AUDITIONS IN PROGRESS. ENTER QUIETLY. "Now, come on."

Gail followed Suzi through the door and looked around. They were in a large open loft with exposed brick walls and a high ceiling. Three huge windows took up most of one wall, and four girls were sitting on the sills, swinging their legs and talking together. Two of them had guitar cases and all of them were dressed in the kind of hip clothing Gail had seen on the kids in the street—lots of denim and leather and multicolored razor-cut hairstyles.

The real action though, was in the center of the room, where a four-piece rock band was tuning up. The drummer, bassist, and keyboard player were all male, but there was a teenage girl with an electric guitar standing behind the center mike. Nearby, an older man, around thirty years old, with stylish blond hair and a crisp white shirt, was adjusting the levels on a sophisticated-looking tape deck.

Suzi walked over to the windows and took a seat on one of the sills. Gail slipped off her jacket and backpack and leaned against the wall, a little apart from the other girls and feeling that way too. In her stiff new jeans and pink cable-knit sweater, she felt decidedly out of it. Besides, she was the only black person in the room, a condition that still felt strange to her, despite four weeks of going to a practically all-white high school.

Gail watched as the blond man stepped around the tape deck and faced the girl at the front of the band. "You're Robin Quinn, right?" As soon as he spoke the whole room fell silent.

"Right," she answered, her voice cracking.

"Good. Now, as you know, I'm starting an all-girl band. The idea is to perform around New York, get some publicity, then take it from there. We'll discuss the business details later—*if* you pass the audition, that is." He paused and took a breath. "All right. Play me something."

Gail watched as Robin announced, "This is a song I wrote. It's called 'You Can't Stop Me Now.'"

As Robin strummed the first chord, Gail felt an odd shiver pass through her. This was the first time she'd ever heard an electric guitar, live and unaccompanied, and she wasn't sure how to react. The sound was so different from the classical music she was used to—louder, scratchier, more raw and bold.

Robin started singing, but Gail was still listening to the sound of the guitar, a steady twang that blasted out of the speakers and filled the room. When the song ended, Suzi leaned over and whispered in Gail's ear, "She's good." Gail nodded, still watching as the band began a steady blues pattern and the blond guy instructed Robin to improvise a solo.

Gail wanted to go on listening, but Suzi kept talking, speculating on her chances of passing the audition, the age of the other girls in the room, and the credentials of Reg Barthwaite, the blond guy behind the tape deck. "I think he produced the last Bob Seger album," she whispered excitedly. "Or was it Tom Petty?"

The names meant nothing to Gail, but she smiled and nodded. Robin was taking off her guitar now and getting ready to leave. Gail had a sudden urge to follow her, to compliment her on her guitar playing. But before she could make a move, Reg's voice broke in. "Next!" he called impatiently. "Where's Suzi Lyle?"

"Here!" shrieked Suzi, grabbing Gail's arm and dragging her across the room.

Reg turned to look at them. "You're a singer, right?"

"Right," Suzi nodded.

Reg looked at Gail. "And who are you?"

"I'm not auditioning," she answered shyly. "I'm just playing piano for Suzi."

Suzi took her place behind the microphone and Gail walked hesitantly toward the electric piano. A tall, frizzy-haired guy stood behind it, eyeing her suspiciously. "Don't screw up my controls," he muttered. "And don't touch the synthesizer."

"Don't worry," she answered. "I wouldn't even know how." Taking her place behind the keyboards she set up the music Suzi had given her and played a few experimental chords. The result was surprising—louder than she'd expected and much more electronic-sounding than the acoustic piano she played at home. The keyboard was smaller, too, and required a lighter touch. Even stranger was that there was no bench to sit on, and Gail had never before played standing up.

But there was no time to worry about that now. Reg was fooling with the controls on the tape deck. "Let's go," he said impatiently. "We're on a tight schedule here."

Obediently Gail began to play. Years of piano recitals had taught her to be at ease in front of an audience, and besides, she reminded herself, with music as simple as this, there was no reason to be nervous. Effortlessly she plunked out the chords with her left hand and added a few embellishments with her right.

Suzi began to sing, something about "It's so easy to fall in love," but Gail wasn't listening. She was enjoying the sound of the electric piano and the pleasant progression of the chords. Like a Scarlatti sonatina, she thought. Simple but nice.

When the song ended, Gail looked up. To her surprise she found that Reg was staring at her. A small smile played around the corners of his mouth as he said, "Try that again. But this time, really let it rock. You know what I mean?"

"Not really," Gail answered honestly. "I'm a classical musician. I never listen to rock 'n' roll."

Reg laughed. "I should have guessed." He glanced into the corner where the male musicians were standing around, smoking and talking. "Bill, Mario, get over here. I want drums and bass on this song." The two men ground out their cigarettes and strolled over. "Okay, now play it again. And you—what's your name?"

"Gail. Gail Harrison."

"Gail. Just listen to the beat and get into it. Let's go."

Instantly the drummer began laying down a solid 4/4 beat. A measure later the bass player picked it up, weaving a string of deep, funky notes underneath. Gail closed her eyes and began to play. With the drums and bass behind her the whole feeling was different, and instinctively she began to syncopate her part, fitting the chords into the musical groove. The sound she was hearing was as foreign to her as an Indian raga, but she had to admit she liked it. When Suzi started singing, Gail broke into a joyous smile. She felt good!

"Okay, okay," Reg said loudly. "That's enough."

Reluctantly Gail opened her eyes and lifted her fingers from the keyboard. "We're way behind schedule," he continued. "Let's get the next girl up here. Linda Belinsky? Let's go!"

Gail walked slowly away from the electric piano, feeling like a little kid who'd just had a new toy taken away from her. Grabbing her backpack and jacket, she followed Suzi out the door.

"Boy," Suzi said irritably. "Thanks a bunch. Reg was so busy teaching you how to play rock 'n' roll that he barely noticed me."

Gail looked anxiously into Suzi's angry face. "I'm sorry," she said. "I didn't realize. I did my best, but I told you I don't know how to play that kind of music."

"Oh, never mind," Suzi muttered as they stepped out into the street. "I'm probably not good enough to join a band anyway."

Gail smiled sympathetically. "Listen, my brother's picking me up at Lincoln Center. Do you need a ride?"

"No thanks. I'm meeting some friends in the Village. You know Tom Bernstein and Bob Ridge? They're on the football team."

Gail shook her head and wondered if she'd ever make friends at her new school. So far Suzi was the only girl she'd said more than ten words to, and that was only because they sat next to each other in orchestra.

"Well, so long." Suzi lifted her fingers in a quick wave. "See you in school."

Gail watched as Suzi walked away. Then she zipped up her jacket, hitched her backpack over her shoulder, and headed over to Canal Street to catch the subway. As she walked, she thought about the rock music she'd just heard—the twanging electric guitar, the thumping beat of the bass drum, the funky pop of the bass. She remembered the feel of her fingers on the keyboard, pounding out a string of syncopated seventh chords.

The music had made her happy, and Gail's first impulse was to hurry home and tell her family. She wanted to explain to them how good the music had sounded as it blasted out of the speakers and filled Reg's empty loft. For a moment she even imagined herself trying out those sounds on her piano at home.

But an instant later she knew it would never happen. Her parents just wouldn't understand. In fact, they'd be downright shocked. To them the only music that mattered was classical. Rock, soul—even Frank Sinatra—just didn't count.

Well, Gail consoled herself, it's not important. This afternoon was my first and last experience as a rock musician. If I'm going to get into Juilliard I don't have time to be fooling around with that kind of stuff. And I *do* plan to get in.

At the next corner Gail crossed the street and headed down the stairs to the subway. When her train came, she took a seat near the door and pulled a book of Beethoven's sonatas out of her backpack. Turning to the first page of the *Appassionata* and began looking over the passages that were giving her trouble.

At first Gail found it difficult to concentrate. The clatter of the subway train sounded like a drum roll and the squeal of the brakes reminded her of Robin's electric guitar. But as she continued to stare at the music on her lap, the haunting minor chords of the sonata took over, gradually filling her head and her heart. With a deep sigh Gail closed her eyes and let the music take control.

 3

"Annette, hurry up! It's starting!"

Annette Giraldi grabbed two cans of soda from the refrigerator and ran into the living room just in time to see the opening credits of *Beach Blanket Bingo* roll across the television screen. Handing a soda to her mother, she took a seat on the sofa and settled down to watch the film.

Annette tried to concentrate, but it wasn't easy. She had seen every old Frankie Avalon–Annette Funicello movie ever made, some as many as five times, and she knew most of the dialogue by heart. Still, she didn't like to disappoint her mom.

Annette took her bubblegum out of her mouth, stuck it on the top of her Coke can, and took a sip. On the screen Frankie Avalon was simultaneously surfing and singing. Annette glanced over at her mother. Her eyes were glued to the screen and she was mouthing the words along with Frankie.

"Your father took me to see this movie when it first came out," Mrs. Giraldi said dreamily. "It was the summer of 1965, I think. We went to the View Point Drive-In." She sighed. "Your father was so handsome in those days, just like Frankie Avalon."

"I know." Annette had heard this story before. Staring at Frankie Avalon's slender body, she found it difficult to see the resemblance between him and her overweight, balding father. Even twenty years ago she was sure he'd never looked that good.

Mrs. Giraldi grabbed her daughter's arm. "Here she comes. Isn't she lovely?" Annette watched the screen as Annette Funicello walked across the beach wearing a tight bikini and sunglasses. "When you were born," Mrs. Giraldi told her daughter, "I took one look at you and said, 'That's my little Annette.' You had the same dark eyes, the same smile." She glanced lovingly at her daughter. "And you're just as beautiful too."

Annette had to laugh. As far as she could tell, she looked absolutely nothing like Annette Funicello. Sure, she thought, we both have dark hair and brown eyes, but that's where the similarity ends. My dumpy body is a laugh compared to her curves. And I would never have the nerve to wear a bikini!

"Don't laugh," Mrs. Giraldi chided her. "You're a beautiful girl. If you'd just get out of those jeans and put on a dress once in a while. Now, when I was going out with your father . . ."

Mrs. Giraldi was off on another of her reminiscences, but Annette just popped her gum back into her mouth and smiled. Sometimes she wished she could escape as easily as her mother did. All it took was a romance novel or an old movie and she was off again, lost in her own private dreams.

Annette stopped smiling when she heard the front door open. They were back. She looked up as her brother, Louis, ran into the room, still wearing his football helmet. "Dad's teaching me how to fake a handoff."

Mrs. Giraldi smiled. "That's good, dear. Now go wash your hands."

As Louis left, Annette's father limped into the room. He was wearing an undershirt and the pants from his police uniform. My dad, the hero, Annette thought bitterly. It's been over six months since he got shot in the leg during that bank robbery, but he never lets anyone forget it.

Mr. Giraldi held the football in one hand and a Budweiser can in the other. "That boy sure does love football," he said proudly, taking a sip of beer. "I wouldn't be surprised if he developed into a first-string quarterback someday."

When no one answered, Mr. Giraldi took another gulp of beer. "How 'bout some lunch?" he said loudly. It was more a demand than a question.

Instantly Mrs. Giraldi jumped up from the sofa. Annette felt her muscles tense. "Can't you see Mom's busy?" she told her father. "Why don't you get it yourself?"

"No one asked you, young lady," her father retorted.

Mrs. Giraldi flipped off the television and glanced anxiously between her husband and her eldest child. "Let's not argue," she urged. "I'm happy to do it."

"Hear that?" Annette's father asked her. "It's only natural for a woman to make food for her husband. If you ever hope to get married, you're going to have to learn that."

"I'd rather die single," Annette muttered, "than marry someone like you."

Mr. Giraldi glared at his daughter. "It's about time you learned your place in the world, young lady. You're a female and you'd better start acting like one, at least while you're in my house."

With that he turned and walked down the hall to the bathroom. A moment later Annette heard the door close and the shower being turned on. "Mom . . ." she began, but Mrs. Giraldi shook her head.

"I think I'll make some tuna salad," she said. "You both like that." With her head bowed she hurried off to the kitchen.

Alone in the living room Annette turned the television back

on and flipped the channels to MTV. A Rolling Stones video was playing and Annette reached for the drumsticks that were lying on the end table. Using the sofa as her drum set, she pounded away in time to the music. As she played, she ground her gum and tried to cool down.

If only that all-girl band thing would come through, she thought longingly. The audition had gone well, but still, the odds of making it had to be pretty small. A few more days, she told herself. I'll give it a few more days. Then I'll just forget about it.

On the television screen the Stones were singing about "waiting on a friend." Annette hit her throw-pillow cymbal and imagined herself playing in a real band. Her father couldn't very well laugh at her drumming then. Not if she was actually performing, maybe even making some money—really out there proving that girls could do anything, even play rock 'n' roll.

"Stop that pounding!" Annette looked up to see her father standing in the doorway, drying his hair with a towel.

"It's only the sofa," she protested. "If I can't have my drums here, at least—"

"And turn off the television," he added. "Lunch is almost ready."

Annette threw her drumsticks onto the sofa and did as she was told. Normally she would have put up a fight, but right now she was too hungry to bother. The phone was ringing as she walked into the dining room. "Just a minute," she heard her mother saying. "She's right here."

"Me?" Annette asked uncertainly.

"Yes, dear." Mrs. Giraldi handed Annette the phone and then carried the bowl of tuna salad into the dining room.

"Hello?"

"Annette Giraldi?"

"Yes?" It sounded like Reg Barthwaite and Annette felt her heart hit a drum roll.

"You passed the audition," he said. "First rehearsal is tomorrow afternoon at three. Same place as the audition. Come ready for some hard work. Understand?"

"Oh!" she gasped. "I can't believe it. I—"

"See you then." There was a click and the line was dead.

Annette dropped the receiver and let out a whoop of joy. Rushing into the dining room, she found her whole family sitting around the table staring at her. Louis held his glass of milk poised in front of his lips, and five-year-old Amy stared at her wide-eyed.

"What is it?' Mrs. Giraldi asked anxiously. "Is anything wrong?"

"I passed the audition!" Annette shouted. "I'm in the band!"

Her father frowned. "What are you talking about? Sit down and eat."

"The all-girl rock band. Don't you remember? I told you about the audition. I saw an ad in *The Village Voice* and—"

"Oh, Annette," her mother said, "I don't like the idea of you going into that part of the city. There's nothing but warehouses in that neighborhood. Couldn't you join a band here in Brooklyn?"

Mr. Giraldi shook his head. "I don't want that music around here. And I don't like the idea of my daughter getting involved with a bunch of Greenwich Village hippies. If you need to hear that kind of music, why can't you go to the CYO dances like the other girls?"

Annette slammed her hand on the dining room table, rattling the dishes and silverware. "You don't understand! You never do!"

"Don't raise your voice, young lady," her father growled. "Sit down and eat."

"Forget it! I'm leaving!" Before her father could respond, Annette ran around the table and out of the room. Grabbing her leather jacket from the coat tree, she left the house, slamming the door behind her.

Out on the sidewalk Annette started running. The streets were an obstacle course of Saturday shoppers, little kids with jump ropes, and women pushing baby carriages. She swerved around them all and turned onto Court Street, never slowing down until she'd reached the high school. Striding swiftly up the steps, she pounded on the doors and waited impatiently for one of the janitors to let her in. "Where's the fire?" he asked, but Annette just shrugged and jogged off down the hall to the auditorium.

Thank God for Mr. Rossner, she thought gratefully, picturing her band conductor's smiling face. Thanks to him Annette had been given permission to keep her drums in the backstage storage closet. He'd even arranged for the janitors to let her in so she could practice on weekends.

Still breathing hard, Annette dragged out her drums and set them up in the middle of the stage. Sitting behind them she breathed a sigh of relief. "I passed the audition," she said out loud, her voice echoing in the empty auditorium. "I'm in the band!"

Picking up her drumsticks she tore into a wild, high-powered drum solo. The cymbals gleamed in the dim light and the drumsticks were a blur in her hands. Annette chomped on her gum and grinned. She had passed the audition! From now on everything was going to be fine.

 4

The footsteps were getting closer. Quickly C.C. stuffed the last piece of clothing into her bag and zipped the top, just as the door opened and her mother breezed into the room.

"Catherine, dear," Mrs. Collins announced, "I'm off to get my hair done. Why don't you come along and afterward we can begin our search for the perfect gown."

C.C. tossed her long blond hair behind her shoulders and let out a weary sigh. "Mother, I thought we'd been all through this. You're the one who's excited about this debutante stuff, not me. Just pick out whatever you want me to wear and buy it. I really couldn't care less."

Mrs. Collins frowned. "Catherine," she said in a pained voice, "I just don't understand you. Not everyone is lucky enough to have a coming-out party. I should think you'd be thrilled."

C.C. didn't know what to say. Ever since they'd moved to Short Hills two years ago, all her parents talked about was "doing the right thing" and "moving in the right circles" and "being accepted." They'd bought a big house, they'd sent C.C. to an expensive girl's prep school, they'd thrown elaborate parties—all for the purpose of meeting "the right people." Now, along with ten other families, they were throwing a big coming-out party at the Hillsbrook Country Club to "introduce C.C. to Short Hills society."

"Mother," C.C. protested, trying to use logic her mother would understand, "what's the point of taking everything so seriously? So I'm having a coming-out party. Big deal. Anyone with a lot of money can do that. The daughters of *real* society families come out at one of the 'invitation only' balls in Manhattan. We'll never be accepted by those people, so why bother? We're just nouveau riche to them."

Mrs. Collins winced at the label. "Old money has to start somewhere, Catherine," she answered. "Your father's success will someday be passed on to your children."

"Fat chance!" C.C. said bitterly. "He'll probably get remarried and have a whole bunch of kids with names like Buffy and Kip and leave all his money to them."

"Young lady, that's enough!"

C.C. didn't want to say any more anyway. Thinking about her parents' separation was just too painful. How could her father have just up and left them like that? Her mother said he was seeing one of his clients—a wealthy young widow who lived in Connecticut. Would marrying her raise his social standing? she wondered. Was that why he'd left?

C.C. shook her head, pushing the thought aside. Tossing her

bag over her shoulder she took a step toward the door. "I'm late, Mother. I have to leave."

Mrs. Collins adjusted her glasses and looked closely at her daughter. C.C. was dressed in a gray skirt, a white turtleneck embellished with tiny pink hearts, and a navy-blue monogramed sweater. "You look darling in that sweater." She smiled. "Where are you off to this afternoon?"

"SoHo. It's the band's first rehearsal." She hurried past her mother and started down the hallway.

"Catherine, get back here!" her mother cried, scurrying after her. "You know I disapprove of this whole thing. It's completely inappropriate. If anyone at the country club found out my daughter was in a rock 'n' roll band, I'd just die."

C.C. stopped at the front door. Dinah, the cleaning woman, was in the foyer, dusting one of the marble sculptures. "Look," C.C. said in exasperation, "after all the money Daddy's contributed to that country club, they wouldn't care if I became a stripper!"

Mrs. Collins stared with horror at her daughter and simultaneously tipped her head to indicate that Dinah was listening. She mouthed the words *Not in front of the servants,* then shot C.C. a stony smile. "Have a lovely time, dear," she said. "And be sure to call if you won't be home for dinner."

Free at last, C.C. walked out the front door and got into the silver Mercedes. Backing down the driveway, she paused to light a cigarette and turn on the radio. At the first stoplight she leaned over and shook her head until her long blond hair was a mass of wavy tangles. There, she thought, running a hand through her bangs until they stood up in fluffy spikes. That's better.

It was a beautiful autumn day—warm in the sun, but with a crisp breeze that made it chilly in the shade. C.C. drove fast, eager to put the tree-lined streets of Short Hills far behind her. At the first gas station on Route 78 she pulled over and walked into the ladies' room. Quickly she unzipped her bag and turned it over. A pile of clothes fell onto the floor, and in an instant she was peeling off her skirt and sweater and slipping into a new outfit. When she'd finished, she stuffed her old clothes into the bag, applied a quick coat of makeup, ran some styling mousse through her hair, and left.

Few people would have suspected that the girl who walked out of the ladies' room was the same one who had gone in only minutes before. In her red leather jacket and black miniskirt she looked older and a good deal wiser. A wild mane of hair bounced around her shoulders, silver hoops dangled from her ears, and she slid into her car with the grace of a professional model. Catherine Christine Collins had been left behind. She was C.C. now, and she was ready to rock.

As she drove away, heads turned and the gas station attendants looked up from the pumps to whistle at her. C.C. just smiled. She knew men were attracted to her and she liked it. It was exciting to know that they were looking at her, thinking about her, wanting to get close. Sometimes it could be scary, too, feeling their eyes on her and wondering what would happen if things went too far. But that was part of the excitement, and as long as she kept moving she felt okay.

Twenty minutes later C.C. drove out of the Holland Tunnel and into SoHo. It was early when she got there, so she parked on Houston Street and walked to the warehouse, checking out the store windows on West Broadway as she went. When she turned onto Greene Street it was still only two-thirty and no one answered when she rang Reg's bell. Taking a seat on the front steps she pulled out a hand mirror and began touching up her makeup.

"Hi!"

C.C. looked up to see a husky girl in a black leather jacket. "Hi," she replied uncertainly.

"Are you here for the band rehearsal? At Reg Barthwaite's place?"

"That's right," C.C. replied, "but he's not here yet. Are you in the band too?"

"Uh-huh." Annette took a seat beside C.C. on the steps. "What instrument do you play?"

"None. I sing."

"I'm a drummer," Annette told her. "I guess that's obvious," she added, flexing a well-developed bicep and smiling. "I've never played in a band, though. Just school stuff—orchestra, jazz ensemble, all that."

"I've been in a few bands," C.C. replied. "On and off."

Annette nodded. "To tell you the truth, I'm a little nervous." She paused and looked at C.C. "I'm not that good a drummer and, well, I don't look like you. I keep thinking that once Reg gets a second look at me, he'll tell me to get lost."

C.C. shrugged. "I'm not worried." She smiled and tossed her hair out of her face. "Reg never took his eyes off me, so I knew I must be doing something right."

Annette didn't respond. For a moment she just stared down at her boots and chewed her gum. Then, abruptly, she stood up and said, "I think I'll go get a soda."

C.C. watched as the girl in the black leather jacket walked off down the street. She wished now that she hadn't acted so cocky, but what else could she do? She didn't even know that girl. How could she admit to a complete stranger that the only singing she'd ever done was in her prep-school glee-club? Besides, C.C. reminded herself, what do I have to worry about? Like I told that girl, Reg likes me. I could see it in his eyes. And as long as that look stays there, I'm in.

C.C. went back to fixing her makeup, but paused when the persistent honking of a car horn caught her attention. Looking up she saw a beat-up black Cadillac cruising down the street toward her. As it came closer, C.C could see that the car was filled with boys. The radio was blasting and someone threw a beer can out the back window.

"Hey, baby!" The Caddy screeched to a halt and a boy with greasy black hair and a tattooed rose on his arm stuck his head out the window. "You look good, honey. Wanna go for a ride?"

Instinctively C.C. tilted her head and smiled. "Thanks," she said, "but no thanks."

"Come on," urged another. "We've got a six-pack."

"Sorry. I'm waiting for someone."

"Stand up!" the driver shouted. "Let's see those legs!" C.C. laughed and shook her head. "Come on! You're beautiful!"

"Why won't you come riding with us?" another boy asked. "We'll just go around the block and bring you right back."

"Oh, sure," replied C.C. "I'll bet."

"What's the matter?" demanded the first boy. "Don't you believe us?" He opened the car door and held out his beer can. "Have a drink. Come on."

C.C. shook her head but the boy with the tattoo stepped out of the car and started walking toward her. For the first time since the car had appeared, C.C. felt nervous. She considered running away, but then decided against it. After all, she told herself, there's nothing to be afraid of. Flirting is fun. It feels good. Besides, they'll get bored in a few minutes and drive away.

C.C. stood up and the boys in the car let out a cheer. The kid with the tattoo leered at her. "Come on, baby," he said smoothly. "Let's go for a drive."

C.C. cocked her head. "Why should I?"

Suddenly the boy lunged forward and grabbed her arm. " 'Cause I said so," he grunted, dragging her toward the car.

"Stop it!" C.C. shrieked. "Let me go!" Frantically she looked up and down the street. No one was in sight.

Before she could scream again, two more boys were beside her, laughing drunkenly as they pulled her across the sidewalk. The driver revved the engine. "Oh, yeah!" he shouted exuberantly. "Bring her here!"

"Let her go!"

Everyone froze. C.C. looked up to see Annette running down the sidewalk, fists in the air. Quickly, while the boys were distracted, C.C. pulled away and took off, running as fast as she could manage in her tight miniskirt and high-heeled boots.

"Get her!" the boy with the tattoo shouted.

"No!" commanded the driver. "Get in here before someone calls the cops. Let's go!" The boys jumped back in the car and a moment later the Cadillac took off, burning rubber.

At the sound of squealing brakes, C.C. turned and simultaneously tripped and fell onto the sidewalk. Before she could move, Annette was beside her. "What happened?" she asked, helping C.C. to her feet.

"I—I don't know," C.C. answered, tears welling up in her eyes. "I was just fooling around, flirting a little. I didn't think they'd try to drag me into the car."

"Are you crazy?" Annette asked incredulously. "You can't go around flirting with boys like that!"

"They seemed okay." C.C. sniffed. "I don't know. It was just a game."

"Some game!" Annette cracked her gum. "Never mind. Come sit down. Did you hurt yourself?"

"No," she answered. "I'm okay." She pulled out her mirror and looked at herself. "Oh, no! My eye makeup is ruined!"

Annette burst out laughing. C.C. tried to look offended, but a second later she gave up and joined in. "Listen," she said between giggles, "thanks for helping me. If you hadn't come along, I could have been in big trouble."

Annette cracked her gum. "You haven't been around much, have you?"

"Sure I have," C.C. answered indignantly. "I come into the city every weekend. I know my way around."

Annette smiled knowingly. "From now on you've gotta be more careful. You shouldn't even talk to guys like that." She looked C.C. over. "You know, I don't even know your name. I'm Annette Giraldi. From Brooklyn," she added, "as you can probably tell from my accent."

C.C. smiled. "Catherine Collins. C.C., that is. I live in New Jersey. Short Hills." She looked down at the sidewalk. "And, Annette, one more thing."

"Yeah?"

"I lied when I told you I'd been in a band before. I never sang in anything except a dumb little prep-school chorus. And if you want to know the truth, I'm scared to death."

Annette looked at C.C. and smiled. "We'll do all right," she said, "as long as we stick together."

‖‖‖‖‖‖‖‖‖‖‖‖‖‖‖‖‖ **5**

Annette and C.C. were still sitting on the steps when Robin showed up. She was wearing faded jeans and an NYU sweatshirt and she carried her battered guitar case protectively under her arm. " 'Scuse me," she muttered, stepping around the girls and starting up the steps.

"Hey," C.C. asked, "are you in the band too?"

Robin turned, her brown curls bouncing against her forehead. "The all-girl band? Yeah. Are you?"

Annette nodded. "Reg isn't here yet. We're keeping the step warm until he shows up."

Robin came down and took a seat. "My name's Robin. Robin Quinn."

"I'm Annette and this is C.C. Soon to be famous as the drummer and lead singer of this band." She motioned toward Robin's guitar case. "What kind of guitar do you have?"

Robin opened her case and lifted out her battered black Fender Telecaster. "You know, this is how Elvis Costello got his record contract," she said, strumming a chord. "He sang on the street outside the building where a Columbia Records convention was going on."

"Who knows," said C.C., "there might be a record company executive around here right now." She pointed across the street to an old man walking his dog. "Hit it, Robin! That's him!"

Giggling, Robin jumped up and started strumming the introduction to her latest song. Without an amplifier the guitar was almost inaudible, but no one seemed to care. C.C. leapt to her feet and danced up the steps while Annette slapped out the rhythm on her thighs.

Rotating her hips like a female Elvis Presley, Robin sang, "You can't stop me now! No, you can't stop me now!"

"Well, well, well." At the sound of Reg's voice the girls froze. He was standing in the sidewalk with his hands on his hips and his head cocked to one side. "What's this?" he asked with a smirk. "Amateur night at the YWCA?"

Robin shrugged. "We were just fooling around."

"Well, I appreciate your enthusiasm, but I'd rather you saved it for rehearsals. Now, let's get upstairs. We've got a lot of work ahead of us."

Silently the girls followed Reg into the building. Inside the loft they took off their jackets and looked around. The room seemed even larger today, and without the noise and excitement of the auditions to distract them, it seemed a lot drearier too. The sun filtered through dirty windows, illuminating the scuffed gray linoleum on the floor and the peeling paint on the ceiling. A drum kit and an electric piano were crowded together in the middle of the room, along with two amps and some microphones. The only other furniture was the table that held the tape deck and five or six paint-splattered straight-back chairs.

"Okay, kids," Reg ordered. "Pull over some chairs and listen up."

As the girls dragged the chairs together, the bell rang and Reg walked over to buzz open the downstairs door. Gail walked in a few moments later with her shoulders drooping and her head hung low.

"I—I'm sorry I'm late," she whispered.

Reg straddled his chair and folded his arms across the back. Slowly he pulled out a cigarette and lit it. "Sit down, Gail," he said firmly. Gail did as she was told, barely glancing at the other girls.

"Well," Reg began, "I guess I should start by telling you something about myself. In the ten years I've been in the music business I've done a little of everything—performing, promoting, producing, the works. I suppose I'm best known for producing the Cool's first album. It went to number three on the *Billboard* charts in 1982."

"Gosh!" Robin exclaimed. "That's a great record." Annette and C.C. nodded appreciatively. Gail had never heard of the Cool, but not wanting to show her ignorance, she nodded too.

"Thanks. These days," Reg continued, "I've been getting into personal management. I've handled a few established bands—Pop Top, the Roos—but that's just a sideline. What I'm really interested in is a girl group."

He paused and flicked the ash from his cigarette. "All-girl bands are big news. Just look at the Go-Go's. Their first album went platinum and their second went gold. But since they broke up, the field is wide open."

Reg took a drag of his cigarette and smiled. "That's where you four come in. I see you girls as sort of a junior version of the Go-Go's—the same enthusiasm and energy, but younger, even more fun. You know, sort of a female version of the Monkees."

"The Monkees?" repeated Annette. "Didn't they have a TV series or something?"

"That's right. And I wouldn't be surprised if I managed to negotiate one for you too."

"A television show!" exclaimed C.C. "Wow!"

"Wait a minute," Robin said sharply. "The Monkees weren't a real rock band. They were just manufactured by a bunch of promoters. I mean, they didn't even play their own instruments."

Reg raised his eyebrows. "I see you know something about the history of rock music," he said. "Well, you're right. On the Monkees' early records the producers used studio musicians for everything except the voices. But this is the eighties and people expect a lot for their money. By the time we're ready to make our move you'll be able to do everything from singing and dancing to plugging acne cream on TV."

Annette laughed nervously. "But we've never even played together. What if one of us can't . . . well, you know, what if we're not good enough?"

"I'm not worried." Reg dropped his cigarette and crushed the butt under his heel. "Why? First, because you've got talent. You may not be the new Beatles, but you can all make music. Second, you're young and enthusiastic. And third, you look good together. I can just see the four of you on an album cover." He nodded, pleased with himself. "No doubt about it. You're marketable."

"But what about the business end of things?" Robin asked, moving to the edge of her chair. "Do we have to sign a contract or something? And what happens if one of us wants out?"

Reg held up his hand. "We'll talk about that later. Right now I just want to get you all playing together. Let's run through a couple of songs and see how it sounds."

"But—" began Robin.

Reg glared at her. "I said *later*. Now, come on. Let's get started."

Annette set up the drum set, Gail pulled the electric piano into place, and Robin took out her guitar and plugged it into one of the amplifiers. Instead of helping, C.C. stood to one side and watched Reg as he set up the microphones and fooled with the tape deck. She liked the way he moved and the sound of his voice. He was handsome too—a little like Sting of the Police. Could he really make me a star? she wondered. When Reg looked up, C.C. met his gaze and smiled. He just stared, outlining her body with his eyes. Then slowly he turned away. He likes me, C.C. told herself. A shiver of excitement slid down her spine.

When everything was ready, the girls took their places. Somewhere in the distance a phone was ringing. "Tune up," Reg told them. "I'll be right back." He ran out of the loft, leaving the girls alone.

"Well, what now?" asked Robin.

"I was here when you auditioned, Robin," Gail said eagerly. "I never heard a guitar sound like that before. It was fantastic!"

"Thanks," said Robin, "but it's really nothing special. I just like to turn up the treble and play loud."

"Well, I'm a classical musician," Gail said softly. "Piano and cello mostly. I don't know much about rock 'n' roll, but it sounded good to me."

Annette frowned. "A classical musician? Then how come you auditioned to be in a band?"

Gail lowered her eyes. "I didn't. I just came along with a friend and sat in on piano. When Reg called and told me he wanted me in the group, I couldn't believe it." She laughed ruefully. "Neither could my friend. She was really mad." Gail looked up. "I wasn't even going to come. I shouldn't have, really, but . . . well, I don't know. I kept thinking about that song Robin sang, and the way her guitar sounded and . . . here I am."

"Boy," said Annette, "that must have been some song. Let's hear it, Robin."

Robin shrugged. "It was the song I was singing in the street when Reg showed up."

"I liked that!" C.C. exclaimed. "Go on. Play the whole thing."

Robin smiled gratefully. All her life she'd been trying to convince people to listen to her songs. The kids in her high-school band had refused to play them, claiming no one would hire the group unless they stuck to covers of Top Forty songs.

"Well, here goes. . . ." She turned up the volume and started strumming. When she sang the first line into the microphone, her voice came back at her crisp and clear. "We-ll, I may be crazy, but I got this dream. . . ."

When the song ended and the last chord died away, the girls cheered. "I love it!" cried Gail, her face glowing.

"Teach it to us," said Annette.

"Just play it again," Gail told her. "I can fake it."

"And I can harmonize on the chorus," C.C. added. A tambourine was lying on the floor near the tape deck. She picked it up and shook it.

"All right." Robin tapped her foot. "One, two, three, four—"

With a crash of Annette's cymbal they were off and playing. It was the first time Robin had ever heard one of her songs with a band behind her and it sounded so good she was practically giddy with joy. She bounced in front of the microphone as she sang, "Well, I may be crazy but I got this dream. . . ."

C.C. joined in on the next line. "I'm gonna make the whole world stand up and scream!"

"I gotta find me a place where I belong," Robin wailed. "So don't try to hold me down, cuz I'll be gone, gone, gone!"

C.C. harmonized on the chorus. "You can't stop me now! No, baby, you can't stop me now!"

When the song ended, C.C. threw her arms around Robin. "I love it!" she cried.

Gail giggled and hopped from one foot to the other. Annette played a drum roll. "It's hard to believe we never played together before," Robin said. "We sound good!"

"Better than good!" Annette exclaimed. "Fantastic!"

"Sensational!" C.C. cried.

"An overnight sensation," Gail added with a smile.

Robin laughed. "That would be a great name for a band. Overnight Sensation!"

"Overnight Sensation," C.C. repeated. "Hmm. I like it."

Annette nodded. "It's us, all right."

Just then the door opened and Reg walked back into the room. The girls fell silent and looked down at their feet, like rowdy schoolchildren when the teacher appears. "Jeez," whispered Annette, "I'd practically forgotten about him."

"Did you hear us?" Robin asked shyly.

"Uh-huh." Reg's expression revealed nothing. He stepped behind the tape deck. "Sorry I was gone so long. Now, let's start with something simple so I can see how you sound together. Maybe a Beatles song."

During the next hour Reg made the girls play "I Want To Hold Your Hand" fourteen times. First, he taught each girl her part and had her play it over until it was perfect. Then he added the instruments one by one. By the time they finally played the song together, Robin was sure she could play her part in her sleep. To break the monotony she added a little guitar solo before the last verse. Reg immediately held up his hands for silence. "Just play what I taught you," he said irritably. "No solos."

Annette caught Robin's eye and winked. "I liked playing your song better," she whispered.

"At least it was spontaneous," she agreed.

Gail shifted her weight from foot to foot and looked at her watch. It was almost six o'clock. If she didn't get home soon her parents would be suspicious.

"One more time," Reg said firmly.

By now the only person really enjoying herself was C.C. She was the center of attention and she loved it. Reg told her to stand in front and encouraged her to shake her hips while she sang. "You're the focal point of the band," he told her. "Make eye contact while you sing. That's right. Look at me."

C.C. did as she was told. Reg's steel-blue eyes were staring into hers, making her heart beat faster. She shook her head the way she'd seen the Beatles do in their old movies. Reg smiled.

Just when Robin was beginning to wish the Beatles had never been born, Reg turned off the tape deck. "We've got a lot of work ahead of us," he said. "First of all we need a bass player. You just can't play decent rock 'n' roll without one." He looked at Gail. "You're the most accomplished musician, so you're elected. You can play bass on some songs and keyboards on others. Robin can learn the bass parts on a couple of songs as well. Next week I'll bring a bass and a small practice amp that you can take home and work with. Okay?"

Gail swallowed hard. Learning to play the bass sounded exciting and she knew it wouldn't be too difficult. She could pick up almost any instrument with a little practice. The thing that worried Gail was her parents. She hadn't even told them she was joining a rock group. How could she possibly explain what she was doing with a bass guitar?

"And C.C.," Reg continued, "I want you to learn your way around the piano. Do you have one at home?"

"Are you kidding?" she asked. "I've never played an instrument in my life. All I can do is sing."

"Don't worry. I'll give you some lessons. And you can come here to practice."

C.C. didn't argue. If learning the piano meant spending time alone with Reg, well, why not? Besides, struggling through a few scales was a small price to pay for stardom.

"Also," Reg told them, "we'll be practicing three times a week. Wednesday night, plus Saturday and Sunday afternoons."

Gail groaned. Annette cried, "Now, wait a minute!"

"Listen, girls," Reg said firmly, "if you want this band to succeed, you'll have to do exactly as I say."

"What are you?" Robin challenged. "Our keeper?"

"No, your manager." Reg paused, his cool blue eyes falling on each of them in turn. "Here's the deal," he said. "Each of you signs a contract giving me exclusive rights to manage and merchandise you—and I also get twenty-five percent of everything you make. In return you get the use of all my equipment and this practice loft, plus the benefit of my contacts and expertise."

Annette looked at the expensive Ludwig drums that were spread out around her. Use of all his equipment, she thought longingly. Sounds good.

"I want to think it over," Robin said cautiously.

Reg stared into Robin's eyes. He seemed to be studying her. Finally he looked away and said, "All right. But remember, I'm offering you a chance to be famous. If you're not interested, there are plenty of other girls who'll be happy to take your place. When I say the word, you're going to have to sign or get out."

The girls looked at each other. "Okay," Robin answered for all of them.

"Good. Then that's it for today. See you Wednesday at seven."

Robin put away her guitar and picked up the case. The other girls followed. At the door she paused and whispered, "On Wednesday night let's meet downstairs at six. Just to sort of talk things over. Okay?" The girls nodded, then started down the stairs.

Only C.C. lagged behind. On her way out the door she paused to glance back at Reg. He was leaning against the wall, watching her closely. As their eyes met he smiled and asked, "What's your hurry?"

C.C. felt her heart hammer against her chest. "Nothing. I—"

"Then stick around. I can give you your first piano lesson right now."

C.C.'s knees felt weak. "Terrific," she said, trying to sound casual. Tossing her leather jacket over her shoulder she stepped back inside the room and closed the door.

 6

Robin walked into Washington Square and sat down on an empty park bench. "Hurry up, Matt," she whispered, glancing up at the black clouds that were rolling in over the skyscrapers. Hugging her books to her chest, she looked down the path just in time to see Matt walk out of the NYU student center. As always his broad shoulders and handsome face made her heart leap. Definitely the leading-man type, she thought dreamily. Who'd have guessed he'd ever fall for me?

Robin thought back to the first time she'd seen Matt. He'd come up to her in the Loeb Student Center on the morning of freshman orientation, a look of bewilderment in his clear blue eyes, and asked, "Can you tell me how to get to Astor Place?" When she told him, his grateful smile had made her feel warm all over. The next day he'd asked her out.

Matt spotted her and waved. She met him halfway, and as he leaned down to kiss her, it began to pour. Matt grabbed her hand and together they ran across the park and into a Sixth

Avenue coffee shop. "Two coffees," Matt called as they claimed a booth. He reached across the table and took Robin's hand. "Where were you last night? I tried to call you."

"At our first band rehearsal." Robin leaned forward. "It turns out this guy Reg is a big deal in the music world. He thinks he can turn us into rock stars. I mean, he was talking about record deals, even TV. Can you believe it?"

Matt's eyes widened. "Come on. Really?"

"Really! He even has a big loft in SoHo for us to practice in." She paused, considering. "Only problem is, he seems pretty bossy. Everything has to be his way. And he wants us to sign—"

Robin stopped talking when the waitress appeared with the coffee. Matt ordered a cheeseburger deluxe. "A BLT," said Robin.

"You better eat more than that," Matt said after the waitress had left. "We have to go straight to rehearsal after this."

"Huh? What rehearsal?"

"The Drama Department play. *Manhattan Magic.*" Robin looked at him blankly. "Don't you remember?" Matt asked, his voice rising. "We need musicians and I asked if you could help out. You said yes. The first rehearsal's tonight."

"Oh," Robin murmured. "I'm sorry. I guess I forgot."

"Thanks a lot. I've got the lead in this play, you know. That's quite an honor for a freshman. Or did you forget that too?"

Robin sighed. "I'm sorry, Matt. I guess I'm just preoccupied with this band stuff. I mean, after months of trying to join a band, who'd ever have thought I'd luck into something like this?"

Matt smiled. "I understand. Just make sure you keep Monday, Wednesday, and Friday evenings open. That's when we have rehearsals."

"Matt," Robin moaned, "I know you're going to kill me, but band rehearsals are Wednesday night."

"Well, can't you change it? After all, you promised me first."

Robin shook her head. "Reg said no."

"That's ridiculous. You don't have to listen to him."

"I'm not so sure. He made it pretty clear we either have to play by his rules, or get out."

The waitress brought the food and Matt poured some ketchup on his cheeseburger. "Well," he said reluctantly, "I guess you can just come to play rehearsals on Mondays and Fridays. But you know, Robin, I'm not sure this band thing is a good idea. This Reg guy sounds pretty intense. Besides, we're only freshmen and we're going to be busy enough as it is. If you want to be in a rock group, why don't you just start one on campus?"

"Matt, be serious! Why should I put together a band to play at fraternity parties when in a few months I could be performing on *Saturday Night Live?*"

Matt looked dubious. "Come on, Robin, isn't that a little farfetched?"

"Well, maybe," she admitted. "Still, this could turn out to be my big chance to make it as a musician. I'm not going to quit after only one rehearsal."

Matt sighed. "Okay, okay. It's just that, well . . ." He reached out and took Robin's hand. "Robin, I just met you and it feels like I'm losing you already. Being in a band is fine, but what about us?"

Robin looked into Matt's eyes. "Oh, Matt, that hasn't changed. Really." She squeezed his hand and smiled. "Now, hurry up and finish your cheeseburger. I don't want to be late for the first rehearsal of *Manhattan Magic.* I've got a crush on the leading man!"

Wednesday evening was cold and clear. At six o'clock Robin was pacing up and down Greene Street, waiting for the others to show up. Blowing on her hands to warm them, she looked up and down the street.

Gail was just turning the corner. "Am I late?" she asked as she walked up. "It takes a while to get here from Maplewood, and the trains aren't always on time."

"You live in New Jersey?" Robin asked.

"Yes. We just moved there from The Bronx."

"Sounds like a big change. What's it like?"

Gail paused, considering. "It's all right, I suppose. I haven't made many friends, but then I was never all that social in my old neighborhood either. I think our family was always considered a little strange. While other kids were out on the corner break-dancing, my brothers and I were in our living room, playing string quartets." She smiled. "Now we're in the suburbs and we're still considered strange, mainly because we're the only black family on the block."

"Well, no one in the band thinks you're weird," Robin said firmly.

Gail grinned. "Thanks. Oh, here come C.C. and Annette."

"Hey," Robin called, picking up her guitar case, "hurry up! We haven't got much time."

"Man, it's cold," Annette said with a shiver. "Let's go somewhere warm."

"I've got just the place," C.C. told them. "Follow me."

Huddling together for warmth the girls followed C.C. down the street. A few minutes later she stopped in front of a double set of red doors. A neon sign in the window said THE SOHO SALOON. "This is a really funky place," C.C. told them, reaching for the door. "Everybody comes here. You'll love it."

Robin grabbed her sleeve. "Hold on. I'm not nineteen. They won't let me in."

C.C. laughed. "Relax. I've been in here lots of times and they've never carded me. It's all a matter of attitude. If you act nineteen, you get treated that way."

"But, C.C.," Gail protested. "I'm only seventeen. I've never been in a bar in my life. Maybe we should just go somewhere else."

C.C. rolled her eyes. "What's the matter with you guys? Don't you want a little adventure in your lives? We're rock stars, remember? We're supposed to know all about living on the edge."

"Right now I'm on the edge of frostbite," Annette said through chattering teeth. "Let's just go in." With a satisfied nod

C.C. walked through the door. Annette followed, pulling Robin and Gail in behind her.

Inside it was dark and crowded. An ornately carved wooden bar stretched along one wall, and in the corner a beautiful old Wurlitzer jukebox was playing the Eurythmics' latest hit. The rest of the room was crowded with tables, most of them filled with people drinking and talking. A heavy cloud of cigarette smoke hung over their heads.

"Just follow me," C.C. said over her shoulder. She led the girls through the crowd and sat them down at an empty table.

Blinking uncertainly, Gail looked around. A woman at the bar was wearing a skintight leather dress that was slit up to her hips. In the corner two men with crewcuts were kissing. One of the waitresses had a Mohawk haircut, half orange, half green.

"Stop staring," hissed C.C. "It's a dead giveaway." She turned to Robin. "So what did you want to talk about?"

Robin put her elbows on the table and leaned forward. "I'm not sure exactly. I just wondered what all of you think about Reg and his plans for the band. I mean, he seems okay, but I can't help wondering if he really knows what he's talking about. Do you think he can actually make us rock stars?"

"Why not?" asked C.C. "You heard what he said. He's been a performer, a producer, everything. He must know what he's doing."

"Maybe so," said Annette, "but I just wish he'd let us sing Robin's song. We rehearsed for almost two hours and all we played was 'I Want To Hold Your Hand.' "

"Did you notice how Reg acted when he came back from that phone call?" remarked Robin. "I asked him if he'd heard us playing and he barely answered. I don't think he liked the idea of us doing anything on our own."

"What's wrong with you guys?" C.C. demanded. "Reg is doing us a big favor. A week ago we were just four nobodies. Now we've got a chance to be rock stars. What more do you want?"

"You're right, C.C.," Gail told her. "Still, things are moving awfully fast. How can I sign a contract? I'm supposed to go to Juilliard next year."

"Listen," said Robin, slapping the table for emphasis, "I'm as excited about this band as C.C. is. I just want to make sure I don't end up in a female version of the Monkees."

"You mentioned them before," Gail said, "but I don't know anything about them. What were they like?"

"They were a pop group that was big back in the sixties—four guys brought together by some TV executives to star in a comedy series they'd cooked up. The idea was to turn them into a sort of watered-down version of the Beatles."

"That doesn't sound so bad," said C.C. "They were stars, weren't they?"

"Sure, but no one over thirteen years old took them seriously. Their managers told them what to say, what songs to play, even what clothes they should wear."

"Reg said he wanted us to be junior versions of the Go-Go's," said Gail. "Are *they* any good?"

"You bet," Annette told her. "They were the first all-female band to make it big. They wrote their own songs, played their own instruments. They were great."

"Yeah, but we don't need to be a junior version of anybody," Robin said firmly. "We can come up with our own style. We don't have to copy anybody else."

"Let's order," C.C. interrupted, motioning to a passing waiter. The man stopped and took out his order pad. "Tequila sunrises all around," she said suavely.

Squinting through the smoke the waiter looked slowly around the table. Robin sat up straight and tried her best to look mature. A long moment passed. Gail cleared her throat. "Can I see your IDs?" the waiter said at last.

"Hey, come on," C.C. protested, looking offended. "We're not kids. Anyone can see that."

"No arguments, girls. Just prove to me you're all nineteen and I'll take your order."

A few people at the other tables turned around to see what

was going on. "C.C." Robin whispered, "let's get out of here." She stood up and reached for her guitar case.

"This is ridiculous!" C.C. cried, but she pushed back her chair and stood up too. "I've never been so insulted in my whole life. Come on, girls. We're leaving!"

"That's the last time we patronize *this* dump!" Annette said loudly. She linked arms with C.C. and headed for the door, her head held high. Robin and Gail followed in silence.

Out on the street C.C. lit up a cigarette and eyed the girls with disgust. "It's all your fault, you know. You three look like babies. No wonder he didn't believe you were nineteen."

Robin laughed. "Look who's talking! I've been here lots of times," she said, mimicking C.C., "and I've never been carded."

The girls giggled. C.C. tried to look mad but soon gave up and laughed too. "I know a better bar anyway," she said. "Come on. We'll go over to Canal Street."

"No way," Robin told her. "It's almost seven. We've gotta get going."

"You acted so cool back there," Annette told C.C. as the girls walked back to Greene Street. "I think you just about had that waiter convinced he was wrong."

"You were pretty cool yourself," said C.C. She imitated Annette's alto voice. "That's the last time we patronize *this* dump!"

"Did you see everybody turn and look at us?" Gail asked with a giggle. "I wanted to crawl under the table!"

"Really!" Robin agreed. "Tequila sunrises all around!" she cried imperiously, and they all laughed until tears came to their eyes.

Back on Greene Street, Robin stopped and waited for everyone to get serious. "So, about the band," she began. "The more I think about it, the more I feel we have to stick together. Reg may be the boss, but we want to have some say in this band too. After all, we're the ones making the music." The girls nodded. Encouraged, Robin went on. "Let's talk to Reg and find out some more about his plans for the band. And most of all, let's not sign anything until we're sure we know what we're getting into."

"Right," Gail said eagerly.

"Okay," agreed Annette.

The girls looked at C.C. "Uh, look," she said uncomfortably, "I can't make any promises."

"Why not?" asked Robin. "Don't you think we should talk to Reg?"

"Sure, it's not that. But as far as signing a contract goes . . ."

"Well?"

C.C. stared at them defiantly. "Well, if you really want to know, I already signed."

"What?" gasped Robin. "When?"

"Sunday night after the first rehearsal. After you guys left, Reg gave me my first piano lesson." Actually, C.C. hadn't learned much about the piano. She'd been too busy concentrating on Reg and the feel of his arm against her shoulder as he reached around her to point out the notes. And then, when the lesson was over, the way he'd softly kissed her good-night . . .

"I hope you know what you're doing," Annette said with concern.

"What's with you three?" C.C. asked defensively. "You know, it's not every day someone comes along and offers to make you a star. If you were smart, you'd stop complaining and sign, too, before Reg finds some other girls to take your place."

Robin glared at C.C., then looked away.

"Well," remarked Annette, "so much for solidarity."

"We haven't got time to talk about this now," Robin said tersely. "We're already late."

"So, what are we waiting for?" asked C.C., shooting Robin an icy smile. Tossing her hair behind her shoulders she turned and started up the stairs.

|||||||||||||||||||||||||||| **7**

The rehearsal was almost over. At Reg's insistence the girls were playing the new song he'd taught them just one more time. As the last chord died away, Reg stepped around the tape deck and kicked aside the cables that ran along the floor. "You sound good, girls," he said, lighting a cigarette. "Real good. Now, about those contracts . . ."

"Wait." Robin unplugged her guitar and stepped forward. "I have a complaint. So far all we've played are covers of other people's songs."

"I'll teach you some originals later. I've written a couple I think will be right, and I—"

"But what about Robin's song?" Annette interrupted. "Why can't we sing that?"

Reg shook his head. "Maybe later," he told them. "Right now I want to stick with songs that fit your image."

"Our image?" Gail repeated.

"Sure. Cute . . . fun-loving . . . innocent . . . enthusiastic. . . . You get the idea. Everybody's idea of the girl next door."

"Hold on!" Robin cried indignantly. "How come you get to tell us what our image is going to be? We want some say in this band too."

"Yeah," agreed Annette. "We aren't going to let you exploit us."

Reg raised his eyebrows. "Exploit you? Are you kidding? I've got three record companies interested in you, sight unseen. Two networks want to put you in a TV series. If that's your idea of exploitation, everyone should be so lucky!"

Robin stared at Reg in amazement. "Three record companies? Really?"

"See," C.C. said enthusiastically, "I told you he knows what he's doing."

Reg smiled at her. "C.C., you sounded great today. Keep singing like that and you'll have a hit record out in no time." Turning to the others he said, "I'll see you all on Saturday. Oh, and Gail, I have that bass and amp for you to borrow." He pointed to a guitar case and a tiny practice amp in the corner. "There's an instruction book in the case. Take it home and learn the notes. Then I'll give you some lessons."

Gail nodded weakly. She still hadn't figured out a way to sneak the bass past her parents. Briefly she considered telling Reg she couldn't do it. In fact, she admonished herself, if I had any sense, I'd tell him right now I can't be in the band at all.

But before she could figure out how to begin, Robin walked up. "I was just thinking," she said. "Since Reg wants me to learn the bass, too, maybe we could do it together. I could come over to your house and—"

"Wait!" cried Gail, suddenly seeing the solution to at least part of her problem. "I've got a better idea. Let's keep the bass at your house. I have to come into the city a lot anyway, so it wouldn't be any trouble for me to come over."

"Well, okay, if you're sure. I'd love to have a bass to fool around with. And you can come over whenever you want to. Tomorrow afternoon, in fact."

"Wonderful," said Gail, breathing a sigh of relief. "Thanks, Robin."

Robin shrugged. "I'm the one who should be thanking you."

"Let's go," said Reg, walking up behind them. "I have to lock up. C.C.," he called, "wait up. I want to talk to you."

Robin grabbed the bass, Gail took the amp, and together they walked downstairs. Outside they found Annette sitting on the fender of a parked car. "Here they come," she said when she saw them. "Everybody's idea of the girl next door."

Robin laughed. "Gimme a break! I wanna be a rock star, not Miss America!"

Annette nodded. "Still, it's hard to resist all those promises of record deals and TV shows."

"I still can't believe this is really happening," said Gail. "I feel like I'm going to wake up and find out it's all a dream."

The conversation was cut short when the front door opened and Reg and C.C. walked out. Reg headed off down the sidewalk, but C.C. hurried over to join the girls. "He's giving me a ride home!" she said breathlessly. "He's going to get his car!"

"C.C.," Annette warned, "are you sure you know what you're doing?"

"What's wrong?" she asked indignantly.

"Well, for one thing, he's about fifteen years older than you."

"So? I'm not a little kid, you know."

"Listen," Robin told her, "we're supposed to be a band. A unit. If you start going out with our manager, it's bound to cause problems. How can we stick together if—"

"All this sticking together stuff is your idea, not mine," C.C. retorted. She cocked her head and looked at Robin. "I think you're just jealous because Reg likes me."

"Yuck," said Robin, wrinkling her nose. "Not a chance."

C.C. smiled. "Good." A beat-up white MG pulled up to the curb and C.C. opened the door. Glancing back at Annette, she said teasingly, "Don't worry. You don't have to rescue me this time."

Annette frowned. "I sure hope not."

Easing herself into the car, C.C. closed the door and turned to smile at Reg. "Where to?" he asked, shifting into first gear.

"Short Hills."

"New Jersey? Jeez, that's a long drive."

"Oh, I'm sorry. If it's too far I could just—"

"No problem. I could use a drink first, though. Let's go over to my place and I'll take you home later."

C.C. looked into Reg's cool blue eyes. A prickle of excitement mixed with fear slid down her neck. Her mother, she realized, was out with her lawyer this evening, "mixing business with pleasure," as she put it. She wouldn't be home until late. "Well, all right," C.C. said boldly. "Let's go."

Reg smiled and shifted into second. As he drove, C.C. watched him out of the corner of her eye. He was so much cooler than the prep-school boys her mother was always pressuring her to go out with. They were just carbon copies of their parents—always talking about the parties they'd been to and the people they knew and the Ivy League colleges they were applying to. But Reg was different. He was part of the New York rock 'n' roll scene. He knew the Cool and he probably knew lots of other rock stars too. Maybe Prince or Tina Turner, or even David Bowie! If I stick with Reg, C.C. thought dreamily, I bet I'll get to know them too.

Reg downshifted and turned onto Sixth Avenue. "So," he asked casually, "what do you think of the band so far?"

"It's great," she said enthusiastically.

"And what about the other girls? What do you think of them?"

"They're okay," C.C. answered. "Especially Annette."

"Hmm. That Robin seems like a troublemaker. What do you think?"

C.C. looked questioningly at Reg. "Well, I don't know. . . ."

He reached over and ran his hand over her cheek. "Go on," he said softly. "You can tell me."

C.C.'s face felt hot where Reg had touched it. "Well," she began, "Robin *does* seem a little pushy. She arranged a meeting before the rehearsal tonight and she told us we have to stick together and not let you take advantage of us. Also, she told us not to sign the contracts."

"Hmmm." Reg didn't say anything during the rest of the drive. When he reached his building, he parked in the underground lot and turned off the car. "Here we go," he said, walking around to open C.C.'s door. She got out and followed him to the elevators.

When they stepped out on the fifteenth floor, Reg took her hand and led her to the door of his apartment. Watching him slip his key in the lock, C.C. began to feel a little nervous. This was the first time she'd ever been out with someone so hip, so sophisticated, so . . . *old.*

Of course, she reminded herself, it's not as if I'm completely inexperienced. I've had plenty of dates with high-school boys—even some college kids.

Still, C.C. had to admit, being with Reg was different. The kids she went out with in Short Hills were just teenagers. They took her to parties or over to the country club for a set of tennis. Real tame stuff. But Reg was an adult and he was taking her to his apartment so they could be alone.

Alone. C.C.'s palms felt damp and her stomach was churning. Cool it, kid, she told herself. You want to be here. It's time to grow up.

Reg flipped on the light and motioned C.C. into the room. It was a tiny studio apartment, not much bigger than her bedroom at home. The first thing she noticed was the clutter—the coffee table was covered with half-empty glasses and cigarette butts, and magazines and newspapers littered the floor. Beyond that a large picture window looked out onto the Hudson River and the lights of New Jersey.

"Great view, huh?" Reg said. He motioned toward the couch. "Have a seat."

C.C. pushed aside some papers and sat down. Reg's apartment, she had to admit, was not what she had expected. The furniture looked as if it must have been expensive when it was new, but that was a long time ago. The rya rug was worn and frayed and there were cigarette burns on the arms of the sofa.

Clearing her throat, she wiped her palms on her pink jeans and tried to think of something to say. It had been a lot easier last Wednesday, with a piano between them and Reg reaching around her to plunk out the notes. Now, with nothing special to occupy her attention, she felt tongue-tied. All she could think was, I'm alone with Reg. In his apartment.

Reg put a record on the stereo. "Want a drink?"

"Sure." A drink would help her relax. She watched Reg as he walked over to the kitchen counter. A large brown roach was scurrying along the floor in front of him. Yuck. C.C. took a deep breath and looked out the window.

Reg came back with two tall glasses and sat beside her. She took her glass and drank deeply. Whiskey. "Sorry," he told her, "I ran out of ice."

"That's okay." C.C. took another long drink. She felt a little light-headed. Tossing her hair off her face, she looked at Reg and giggled. He caressed her shoulder and smiled back. She could smell his shampoo and the alcohol on his breath.

"C.C.," he said, "you girls sound good together. In fact, I don't think you realize just how good you are."

"Really?" she asked, blushing with pleasure.

"Yep." He lit two cigarettes and handed her one. For a full minute he just sat there, smoking and gazing pensively out the window. When he finally spoke, it was more to himself than to C.C. "You know," he said softly, "after I did the Cool's first album, I was one of the hottest producers in the business. Everybody wanted to work with me." He paused and took a drag on his cigarette. "But now, well, I haven't had a hit in two years." He turned to C.C. "That's why this band is so important. There's no way you girls can bomb. You're naturals. But, C.C., you've got to promise me something."

"What?" she asked, sipping her drink and thinking proudly, He needs my help.

"Promise me you'll try to convince the other girls to sign the contracts. I could get replacements, of course, but there's something about you four that feels right. You look good, you sound good. It's the right chemistry. Besides, I already sent out publicity photos."

C.C. nodded. "I'll try. I already told them once I thought they should sign."

"You did?" Reg looked pleased. "Good girl." Slowly, he leaned over and kissed her. C.C. kissed back, tasting the whiskey on his lips. He put his arms around her and pulled her close. C.C.'s palms were still damp, but now it was more from excitement than fear. Reg ran his hand through her hair and kissed her ear.

"C.C.," he whispered, "stay with me tonight."

C.C. felt frightened. Relax, she told herself. It's not as if you've never been with a guy before. She thought back to her senior prom. She and Jerry Bennett had practically made it in the backseat of his parents' Porsche. Still, that wasn't the same as spending the night with somebody. Especially somebody as old and experienced as Reg. "I—I can't," she muttered. "My mother'll freak if I don't come home."

Reg stared at her. "I didn't know you still lived at home." He laughed softly. "Jailbait."

"I am *not*," C.C. said indignantly. "I'm eighteen."

Reg smiled and ran his hand lightly over her neck. "Sorry."

C.C. reached for her glass. It was empty. Leaning back against the sofa, she looked out the window. The lights across the river seemed to be moving. They danced and collided, blurring before her eyes. C.C. blinked and tried to make them stop. "What time is it?" she asked, trying to stand up.

Reg grabbed her hand and pulled her back onto the sofa. "Early," he whispered. "I'll drive you home later."

"Well . . ." She closed her eyes and tried to think. On the stereo a soul group was singing something about "the way you do the things you do."

Reg stood up and walked over to the kitchen counter. A moment later he was back with two more drinks. C.C. looked up into his face. She liked his high, sculptured cheekbones and the tiny wrinkles around his eyes. He didn't look anything like the fresh-faced teenagers she was used to dating. Good, she told herself. I'm through with immature preppies. I'm ready to grow up.

Reg handed her a glass and she drank deeply. When she looked up again, he was unbuttoning his shirt. C.C.'s stomach did a somersault. "Reg?" she asked shakily.

"Hmm?"

"Can . . . can you really make me a star?"

"Honey," he said huskily, "I'm gonna do my best." Sitting down beside her, he kissed her long and hard, running his hands down her shoulders and across her breasts. C.C. gasped.

"That's right," he whispered. "Now, just relax." Reg put one hand in the middle of C.C.'s back and pulled her close. With his other hand he reached up and turned off the light.

||||||||||||||||||||||||| **8**

"Gail! Breakfast!"

Gail pulled the crumpled bag out of the back of her drawer and opened it. With growing excitement, she took out her new blouse and held it up. It was the first time she'd looked at it since last Saturday, when Robin had helped her pick it out in Greenwich Village. "You need something to wear with the band," Robin had told her. "Those skirts and pink sweaters are definitely not making it."

"Well, here goes," Gail whispered, slipping the blouse over her head and peeking at herself in the mirror. Next to her nut-brown skin the white cotton seemed to glow, and the artistic splashes of red, green, and yellow paint looked bright and bold across her chest. Hesitantly, she pulled the blouse so that it hung low on one side, exposing her shoulder the way Robin had shown her.

"Gail! Hurry up! You're going to be late!"

Gail carefully adjusted the blouse so that most of her shoulder was covered. Taking one more look in the mirror—it really looked pretty good—she hurried into the kitchen. Gail's mother stood at the kitchen counter, making waffles and skimming over the headlines in the morning paper. At the head of the table her father was glancing through a pamphlet on computers and sipping his orange juice. Eighteen-year-old Jesse, a freshman at Juilliard, was looking over a chapter in his orchestration textbook. And ten-year-old Garrett, the baby of the family, was giggling his way through the funnies.

"Good morning," Gail said softly, slipping into her seat. As on every other morning, she felt a little disoriented. No matter how hard she tried, she still couldn't take the changes in her life for granted. Only six months ago her father had been working at a shipyard and going to night school. Now he wore a suit and tie and worked in an office, programing computers. Gone was their cramped two-bedroom apartment, with its temperamental plumbing and leaky roof. They were in the suburbs now, in a three-bedroom ranch house, complete with wall-to-wall carpeting and a grassy front lawn.

"Gail!" Gail's thoughts were interrupted by her father's stern voice. Timidly she looked up into his wide, dark face. "Where on earth did you get that shirt?"

"I bought it in the city, Daddy," Gail said quickly. "All the girls at school wear them. Isn't it fantastic?"

"Fantastic is not the word I would use. I think it looks gaudy. Gaudy and cheap."

Gail's mother put a plate of waffles on the table and sat down. "Now, John, relax. I'm sure Gail's under a great deal of pressure to conform at her new school. She's different enough as it is. Let's not stop her from trying to fit in."

"She was under pressure to conform in our old neighborhood too. All of us were. But we rose above the things we saw around us."

"Aw, Pop," Jesse broke in, "it's only a shirt."

"That's right," agreed Mr. Harrison. "And when I wanted to get my hair straightened and go down to the pool hall with the other boys, I told my father, 'Pop, it's only a haircut.' But where are those other boys now? They're unemployed and uneducated, still spending their days smoking reefer and playing pool. But not me." He looked at his family with pride. "Not us. We've made something of ourselves."

"John," Mrs. Harrison said gently, "the waffles are getting cold."

"I'm sorry, hon. Sometimes I just get carried away." He patted his wife's hand and reached for the syrup.

"Now, let's all get our schedules straight," Mrs. Harrison told the family. "Your father and I have choir practice at St. Luke's tonight. You have Youth Orchestra this afternoon, right, Garrett? And Gail has her piano lesson."

"That's right," said Gail. "And afterward I'm going over to Juilliard to rehearse with Mr. Dawson's chamber-music group."

"I'm glad Mr. Dawson started this group," Gail's father said, sipping his coffee. "It's sure to count for something on your Juilliard application."

"I just hope it isn't too time-consuming," Mrs. Harrison added. "You seem to spend almost all your time practicing for this recital, Gail."

Gail gulped down a mouthful of waffles. "But I like it," she said eagerly. "And I'm still doing well in school."

"When's the recital?" Jesse asked. "I've been checking the bulletin board at school but I haven't seen a notice."

"I'm not sure," Gail answered nervously. "Mr. Dawson hasn't told us yet."

Mr. Harrison finished his waffle and wiped his mouth with his napkin. "Well, be sure to let us know." He stood up. "I have to run. Gail, I won't say anything more about that blouse. You're old enough to make your own decisions. Just promise me you'll think about what I said. All right?"

"Yes, Daddy."

On the way to the bus stop Gail did just that, and the more she thought about it, the more miserable she felt. *He's upset just because I bought a flashy blouse,* she thought guiltily. *What would he do if he found out I was playing in a rock 'n' roll band?*

Gail sighed. She knew she couldn't go on like this much longer. So far her story about the chamber-music group had worked. But what would happen when a few more weeks passed and she still couldn't tell her parents the date of the recital? They'd probably call Mr. Dawson and find out the truth. There wasn't any chamber-music group. There never had been. It was all a lie, something Gail had made up so she could get out of the house and play rock 'n' roll.

The thought of being found out made Gail's stomach churn. She'd never lied to her parents before. Until she joined the band she'd never had to.

There's only one solution, Gail told herself firmly. I have to quit the band. In fact, I never should have joined in the first place.

When the school bus pulled up, Gail got on and took a seat next to the window. At the back of the bus a group of boys were listening to a portable radio. To her surprise Gail recognized the song that was blasting out of the speakers. It was one of the tunes Reg had taught the band. As the bus rumbled along, Gail closed her eyes and mouthed the words.

The bus hit a bump and Gail felt her blouse slide off her shoulder. Instinctively she reached up to fix it, then changed her mind. The breeze from the open window felt good against her skin.

Gail smiled. When she listened to music like this, anything seemed possible. Even something totally crazy, like forgetting about Juilliard and just devoting herself to the band. She rested her head against the window and sang along with the radio. "Believe in the magic that can set you free. . . ." I do believe, thought Gail. I really do.

Gail walked down Sixty-third Street and turned onto West End Avenue. When she came to Mr. Dawson's building, she stopped and took a deep breath. Nervously she wiped her hands on her pants and tried to concentrate on her lesson for today— the opening section of Liszt's Sonata in B minor—but all that came to mind was a bass line from one of the rock songs the band was learning.

"Oh, why didn't I practice more?" Gail moaned. The answer, she realized, was all too obvious. Between rehearsing with the band and learning to play the bass, she'd hardly had a free moment all week.

Like a prisoner on her way to the gallows Gail walked up the steps and rang Mr. Dawson's bell. In the elevator she thought about how happy her parents had been when Mr. Dawson accepted her as a pupil. "He teaches at Juilliard and gives a few private lessons on the side," they'd told her. "Studying with him will certainly look good on your application."

But to Gail, Mr. Dawson was more than just a good teacher. He was the most talented, the most wonderful, the most beautiful man she'd ever met. She loved his smooth black skin, his dark-brown eyes, his soft baritone voice. Just being in his comfortable, sunny apartment made her happy. And when he played the piano . . . well, it was almost heaven.

That's what made not practicing so awful, Gail thought sadly. Not only was she letting down her parents, she would be disappointing Mr. Dawson as well. And that was almost too horrible to think about.

By the time she reached the eleventh floor, Mr. Dawson was standing in the doorway of his apartment. He was a tall, slender man, with almond-shaped eyes, a long nose, and full brown lips. In his gray slacks and tan V-neck sweater he looked younger than his forty-four years and, in Gail's eyes, breathtakingly handsome. "Hi, Gail," he greeted her. "Come on in and warm up. I've just got to make a phone call."

Gail followed Mr. Dawson into the apartment and took a seat at the baby grand. "Play your scales," he told her as he walked out of the room. "I'll be right back."

Alone in the living room Gail played through the major scales and looked around. She loved the comfortable furniture, the plush rugs with their swirls of color, the framed concert posters on the wall, and the shelves of records. She breathed deeply and tried to relax. Maybe if she stayed calm and really concentrated, the lesson would go all right.

Gail went on to the minor scales. When she'd finished, Mr. Dawson was still on the phone. Glancing guiltily over her shoulder, she stood up and walked away from the piano. She knew she should be using this time to practice her lesson, but she couldn't resist the chance to look around Mr. Dawson's living room. Dreamily she picked up a book of matches from the coffee table and wondered what it would be like to live with Mr. Dawson. Every day would be devoted to classical music—playing the piano, studying scores, listening to records. . . .

An album cover resting near the stereo caught Gail's attention. Walking over, she picked it up. Miles Davis. But wasn't he a jazz musician? Gail walked to the record shelves and looked over the titles. Bach, Mozart, Wagner . . . Louis Armstrong, Charlie Parker, Art Tatum! Mr. Dawson listened to jazz!

"Gail, I thought you were supposed to be warming up."

Gail spun around and found herself face-to-face with Mr. Dawson. "I—I'm sorry," she said timidly. "I was just looking at your records."

Mr. Dawson looked at the album in Gail's hand and smiled. "Miles Davis is a genius. But as a pianist you really have to listen to guys like Art Tatum, Erroll Garner, Thelonious Monk. They're just amazing."

"I didn't know you liked jazz," Gail said wonderingly.

"Of course. I love any kind of music, as long as it's challenging and well played." He gestured toward the window. "There's a whole world of sound out there, Gail. Keep your ears open."

"I—I am," whispered Gail. She looked up into Mr. Dawson's face. If only I could tell him about the band, she thought longingly. Maybe he'd understand.

But what if he didn't? Jazz was one thing, but would Mr. Dawson include rock 'n' roll under the heading "challenging and well played"? And what if he found out about the lies she'd been telling—lies about Mr. Dawson and his imaginary chamber music group?

"Mr. Dawson?"

"Yes, Gail?"

"I . . . I . . ." Go on, she admonished herself. Tell him about the band. But all that came out was "I didn't practice very much this week."

Mr. Dawson's face clouded over. "If you're going to make the piano your career, you must practice regularly," he said sternly. "Do you realize how many teenagers, just like you, dream of being concert pianists? The competition is fierce."

"Yes, sir. I'm sorry."

"No apologies. Just sit down and play me the Liszt."

"Yes, Mr. Dawson." Gail dragged herself to the piano and sat down. With trembling fingers she took out her music and started to play.

 9

"Mother, how *could* you?"

Mrs. Collins put down her glass of wine and looked across the table at C.C. "Catherine, calm down. You were going to the party anyway. I just thought it would be nice if you had a date."

"But I don't even know the guy! Besides, I hate Patty Hawthorne. Why would I want to go to her birthday party?"

"Because you and Patty are coming out together, that's why." Mrs. Collins paused when the maid appeared at the dining room door. "We'll have coffee in the living room, Mary," she said. "Come along, Catherine."

C.C. followed her mother into the living room and took a seat on the white silk sofa. "Who is this guy, anyway?" she asked, propping her feet up on the mahogany coffee table.

"He's Eve Vandenburg's son and—put your feet down, dear." Reluctantly, C.C. obeyed. "Eve and I had lunch together in the city today and she mentioned that Kurt had been invited to Patty's party." The maid brought in the coffeepot and cups on a silver tray and placed it on the coffee table. "Thank you, Mary." Mrs. Collins poured the coffee and handed one to C.C.

"Kurt's father is a full partner in one of the biggest law firms in New York. Bennett, Vandenburg, and Pearson—very prestigious. Eve said Kurt is putting off college for a year and working for his father instead. He wants to get a feel for law before he starts school."

C.C. nodded glumly. She'd seen Kurt Vandenburg around the country club. Medium height, medium build, straight brown hair, and dark-brown eyes. Just another typical preppie. Maybe I can fake a headache or something and get him to bring me home early, she told herself.

"You need three escorts for the deb ball," C.C.'s mother reminded her. "I think Kurt would be a good choice."

"Okay, okay, I get the idea," C.C. muttered. "What time is he coming over?"

"In about an hour." C.C. stood up and Mrs. Collins reached for her hand. "Don't be angry, honey. I just want the best for you. Until your father comes back, it's just the two of us. We have to stick together."

Until my father comes back? Does she know something I don't? C.C. wondered. She thought back to the night he'd moved out. Lying in bed, C.C. had heard her parents arguing downstairs. Her mother had slammed the door and shouted something about "that bitch." The next morning Mr. Collins was gone.

That was almost two months ago and C.C. hadn't seen him since. He'd sent money—lots of it—and a diamond necklace on the day of her high school graduation. He'd even written a couple of letters arranging luncheon dates. But so far he'd never shown up.

"Have you talked to Daddy?" C.C. asked her mother eagerly.

"No, but Eve saw him at the bar in the Ritz last week. She said he was looking very down. I think he'll get over this little midlife crisis and come home soon."

"Sure," C.C. said, trying to keep the disappointment out of her voice. "Well, I better go get dressed."

Upstairs C.C. tried to think of a way to get out of Patty Hawthorne's birthday party. She could pretend she was sick, maybe. She could even flat out refuse to go, but of course that would precipitate a huge fight and a really weird scene when Kurt showed up. Better to just go and get it over with. Maybe the punch would be spiked and she could drink herself into oblivion.

When the doorbell rang, C.C. checked herself in the mirror. She was wearing a navy-blue dress with puffy sleeves and a high lace collar. Her long blond hair was piled on her head in a loose twist. Low navy-blue heels and the diamond necklace her father had sent her completed the picture. Well, thought C.C., it's not a leather miniskirt, but at least my mother will approve.

Downstairs Kurt was sitting on the love seat, chatting with C.C.'s mother. "Oh, there you are!" Mrs. Collins exclaimed. "Come on in and meet Kurt."

Kurt stood up and smiled. "Hello, Catherine," he said politely.

C.C. eyed him warily. He was wearing a gray suit, a light-blue shirt, and a navy-blue knit tie. His dark-brown hair was short and brushed back from his forehead, and his face was good-looking in a youthful Kevin Bacon sort of way. "Hi," she replied.

"Well, have a good time, you two," Mrs. Collins said merrily, standing up. "Stay as late as you like, Catherine. Have fun."

"Okay, Mother. Bye."

Out in the car Kurt turned to C.C. "Blind dates are pretty weird, I know, but, uh, let's try to make the best of this, okay?"

"Yeah, sure," C.C. muttered, unconvinced. Kurt started the car and backed out of the driveway. As they drove, she stared out the window and thought about Reg. How she wished she were going to a music-business party with him instead of an eighteenth birthday party with Kurt Vandenburg! He would introduce her to all the rock stars and put his arm around her and whisper, "You've got more talent than all these people put together."

An image of Reg unbuttoning her jeans popped into C.C.'s mind. She closed her eyes and replayed the scene in her head, just as she'd done so many times since that night. She remembered the feel of his body against hers, his hard chest pressing against her ribs, and his chest hairs tickling her breasts. His breath came in short gasps as he moved on top of her. Then all at once it was over. With a grunt, he rolled away and stretched out on the sofa beside her. A few minutes later, he was asleep. C.C. remembered lying there in the darkness, listening to his steady breathing and whispering over and over, "Reg likes me. He's going to make me a star. . . ."

"It's funny we've never met before," Kurt was saying. "I've seen you at the country club. My dad plays tennis with your dad, you know. At least they used to. I haven't seen your father around much lately."

"My father doesn't live with us anymore," C.C. said flatly. "He moved out two months ago."

"Oh. Oh, I'm sorry. I—I didn't know."

Kurt was obviously flustered, but C.C. didn't feel like bailing him out. An uncomfortable silence settled over the car, broken only when they arrived at Patty Hawthorne's house.

"I hear Patty hired a live band for the party," Kurt said with forced cheerfulness. He pulled into the semicircular driveway that led up to the large white Colonial house. "I wonder if they'll be any good."

C.C. snorted a laugh. "Come on! They'll probably be a bunch of middle-aged guys in tuxedos. You know, the kind of band that's supposed to play something for everyone. That means 'Strangers in the Night' followed by a wimpy version of 'Beat It.' "

Kurt laughed with delight. "I bet you're right. Man, I wish they'd get some decent New York act like Marshall Crenshaw or David Johansen."

"Yeah. Wouldn't that be great?"

"Do you like Marshall Crenshaw?" Kurt asked.

"Well, I liked his first album a lot. 'Someday, Someway' was great and—"

"Right!" Kurt interrupted eagerly. "And didn't you love 'Rockin' Around in N.Y.C.'?"

"Yeah, and 'She Can't Dance.' I haven't heard his second

album, but I—" Suddenly, C.C. stopped, realizing what had happened. She and Kurt were actually talking and laughing together. Could it be he wasn't such a jerk after all? She giggled nervously.

"What's so funny?" Kurt asked, smiling uncertainly.

"Nothing. I guess I'm just surprised you know something about rock 'n' roll. The way my mother talked about you, I figured you'd be a real bore."

"Thanks a lot," Kurt said, pretending to be offended. Then he smiled. "Actually, I do have my boring moments. Like every weekday from nine to five. That's when I put on a three-piece suit and hang out at my father's law office, trying to look like I'm not falling asleep."

"I thought you *wanted* to be a lawyer. Isn't that why you're working there?"

"No way," he replied, shaking his head. "That's my dad's idea. I want to go to art school."

"Art school! Hey, that sounds excellent."

"How about you? Are you in college this year?"

"Nope. My parents said I should wait till next year. This is my debut year, you know," she added sarcastically. "I'm being trained in the fine art of going to parties."

Kurt laughed. "I know what you mean. Practically every girl I know is coming out this year. I've been invited to seven balls already!" He paused and smiled at C.C. "You know, Catherine, I'd love to spend the evening talking to you out here in the car, but don't you think Patty might wonder what happened to us?"

C.C. giggled with embarrassment. She hadn't even noticed they were still in the car. "Oh, sure. Let's go. And by the way, call me C.C. Only my parents call me Catherine."

"Okay, C.C. Let's go." He came around and opened C.C.'s door and together they walked up the steps.

"Happy birthday, Patty," Kurt said when the front door opened. "Welcome to adulthood."

"Oh, thank you, Kurt. Hi, C.C. Let me take your coats. There's food in the dining room and dancing in the solarium. Mummy hired a really super band."

C.C. and Kurt looked at each other and tried not to burst out laughing. "Thanks, Patty," Kurt said, helping C.C. off with her coat. "Come on," he added with a wry smile. "Let's rock."

Kurt offered his arm and together he and C.C. walked through the house to the solarium, a vast room with floor-to-ceiling windows. In one corner a five-piece dance band was making its way through a lumbering version of "Sweet Dreams Are Made of This." The room was crowded with teenagers, talking or dancing to the music. A set of French doors led out onto a large patio strung with lighted lanterns, but the night was chilly and no one had ventured outside.

"What did I tell you?" C.C. said, motioning toward the band. "The pits."

Kurt nodded. "Oh, well, let's grab some food and sit out on the patio. It's too noisy to talk in here."

"Okay. I'm starving."

"Great. Go on out. I'll get some food and meet you there."

C.C. walked through the crowd, smiling and waving to the kids she knew. Pushing open the French doors she stepped out onto the slate-covered patio and looked around. The backyard was cool and dark and filled with the sweet smells of grass and dirt and chrysanthemums. Sitting down on one of the stone benches C.C. closed her eyes and listened to the muted strains of a Glenn Miller tune wafting out from the house.

This music stinks. How can the other kids dance to it? she wondered. She thought back to the band's last rehearsal. Robin and Annette had been complaining that Reg never let them sing Robin's songs. I'd like to sing some of Robin's songs, too, thought C.C. But, after all, Reg is the boss. He knows what's right for the band, doesn't he? She remembered the way he'd smiled at her at the end of the rehearsal. "Keep singing like that," he'd said, "and you'll have a hit record out in no time." A hit record! C.C. tried to imagine what it would be like. Audiences screaming when she walked on stage . . . her name in *Rolling Stone* . . . a video on MTV. And freedom. Freedom to wear whatever she wanted, say whatever she wanted, do anything she pleased. God, it sounded great!

"A slice of quiche Lorraine for your thoughts."

Startled, C.C. opened her eyes. Kurt was standing in front of her, his arms filled with plates of food, napkins, silverware, and two glasses of punch. "Quiche Lorraine?" C.C. asked.

"Well, that's all I have to offer right now. I can't get you a penny unless you take these glasses out of my hands."

Smiling, C.C. took a plate and a glass of punch. "Do you really want to know what I was thinking?" she asked. Kurt sat on the bench beside her and took a bite of quiche. "I was day-dreaming about being a rock star." She laughed briefly. "Sounds stupid, doesn't it?"

"Are you kidding? It sounds great!"

"I'm serious," she said earnestly. "I'm in a band. Our manager used to produce the Cool. He's got three record companies interested in us too."

"Wow, that's fantastic!"

C.C. frowned. "You really think so?" she asked uncertainly. "Most people I know around here are more interested in going to parties and showing their horses than in listening to rock 'n' roll. In fact my mother is totally freaked out by the whole thing. If anyone at the country club finds out I'm in a band, she'll probably have a nervous breakdown."

Kurt laughed. "I know what you mean. My parents want me to be a lawyer like my dad. They practically fainted when I told them I want to be an artist. That's why I'm working at my father's office this year. He wouldn't send me to art school and I wouldn't go anywhere else, so we compromised. I'm learning a few things about corporate law in the daytime and taking a course at Cooper Union at night."

"What kind of art do you do?"

"Crazy stuff," Kurt said with a smile. "That's what most people seem to think, anyway. It's sculpture, mostly. I want to make really big things—total environments—but my parents won't let me do anything larger than what I can fit in my bed-room." He paused, his head cocked toward the house. "Listen, they're playing 'My Funny Valentine.' I love that song." He held out his hand. "May I have this dance?"

C.C. rolled her eyes. "Come on. Do you really like that kind of music?"

"Sure. I like horse shows and country clubs, and coming-out parties too. It's all fun if you don't take it too seriously." He jumped up and grabbed C.C. around the waist.

"Hey!" she cried. "Let go!"

Ignoring her protests Kurt pulled her to her feet and took her in his arms. "There, now, this isn't so bad, is it?" he asked, looking deep into her eyes.

Kurt's hand was covering hers and his arm held her firmly around the waist. She could feel the warmth of his body and smell the sweet scent of his cologne. "No," she murmured. "It feels good."

"Then put your head on my shoulder." Closing her eyes, C.C. rested her cheek against his soft wool jacket and let Kurt dance her across the patio.

It was after midnight when they pulled up in front of C.C.'s house. "Did you have a good time?" he asked, turning to face her.

C.C. thought back over the last few hours and smiled. They'd spent the entire evening dancing and talking, out on the patio at first, and later—after Patty had noticed them and come out to tease them—inside with the others. "Yes," she said. "Yes, I did."

"Can I see you again? Maybe Sunday afternoon?"

Sunday afternoon. The band would be rehearsing then. For the first time in hours C.C. remembered Reg. Just thinking about him made her heart beat faster. That blond hair, those intense blue eyes. God, he was so sexy!

C.C. looked at Kurt. He's cute, sure, but he's so young. Besides, Kurt's into the whole Short Hills scene. Horse shows, country clubs, the whole bit. C.C. shook her head. I've got bigger things in mind, things that only Reg can give me. Sorry Kurt, she said to herself, but I'm going to be a star.

"Gee, I'm really busy with the band right now," she said,

avoiding Kurt's eyes. "Maybe we'll see each other at the country club, or at my coming-out party. . . ."

"Yeah," he answered flatly. "Maybe."

C.C. glanced up at Kurt. She liked his dark-brown eyes and his delicate upturned nose. Maybe I'm making a mistake, she told herself. But then she thought of her mother and how delighted she'd be to hear that C.C. and Kurt had hit it off. Probably the first thing she'd do would be to run to the *Social Register* to see if his family was listed. Well, forget it, C.C. told herself. I'm not into that scene. I'm getting out. "Good night, Kurt," she said firmly, opening the car door and stepping out.

"C.C., wait, I—"

But C.C. had already started closing the door and it slammed shut before he could get out the rest of the sentence. Instinctively she reached out to grab the handle, but Kurt didn't notice. Jamming the clutch to the floor, he put the car in reverse and backed out of the driveway. Their eyes met for just a second, then he shifted into first and drove away.

|||||||||||||||||||||||||| **10**

By the beginning of November the band had been together for almost six weeks. During that time Reg had taught the girls twenty songs, many of them lightweight pop tunes from the sixties by bands like the Grass Roots, the Dave Clark Five, and Tommy Roe. He'd also written some songs himself. One was called "The Boy of My Dreams," a tune he said was perfect for the band's girls-next-door image. Another, "Girl's Rock," was supposed to be the band's theme song. The chorus, which all the girls sang together, went

"When we get the urge, we have to converge,
To make some sound and shake it around,
That's girl's rock!"

After the first few rehearsals Reg had stopped talking about contracts. All he seemed concerned with now was the music and what he called "the look." He made the girls play every song over and over again until they had each note down perfectly, and while they were playing he urged them to dance and smile. "Have fun with it," he shouted. "Think happy! Think cute!"

C.C. had no problem following Reg's instructions. She just kept her eyes on him and did whatever it took to get his approval. But for the other girls, "thinking cute" wasn't always so easy. Annette's smile turned into a grimace the moment she began banging on her drums. Gail had a tendency to hang her head and stare down at her instrument. Robin liked to dance while she played, but Reg didn't like her intense expression. "The audience doesn't want you to bare your tortured soul, Robin," he yelled. "They just want to see some cute girls playing good-time music."

In between songs Reg ran around the room, fiddling with the dials on the tape deck and amplifiers. He even brought in a lot of fancy equipment which no one but Robin understood—a PA, a mixing board, and monitors. The idea, he explained, was to find "the perfect sound"—the sound that the world would instantly recognize as C.C., Robin, Annette, and Gail.

But Reg's idea of the perfect sound was different from what the girls had in mind. Reg used equalizers and noise reduction equipment to make everything sound sweet and smooth and pretty. He refused to let Robin turn up the treble on her guitar and forced Annette to leave out the fancy drum fills and just keep the beat.

"This is boring!" Robin protested. "We want to turn up the volume and rock out."

"No way," Reg replied. "Loud rock music only gets played on rock 'n' roll radio stations. I'm going to create a sound that everybody wants to hear. Rock fans, easy-listening fans, even country fans—they'll all be crazy about you."

Then one Saturday, Reg ended the rehearsal a half hour earlier than usual. "I've got some good news for you, girls," he announced with a smile. "I've arranged a showcase performance for you on December tenth at the Supermarket. Everyone who's shown interest in you is going to be there—record and TV people, reporters, photographers, the works. You're going to show them what you can do, and then we'll wait for the offers to roll in."

"The Supermarket?" repeated Robin, awestruck. All the best bands in town played the Supermarket! In fact, the last time Robin had been there she'd seen the Pretenders.

"Of *course* the Supermarket." Reg chuckled. "I told you I was going to make you famous, and I meant it. But don't forget, girls, this is a business venture. I supply the money and the know-how, you supply the talent, and the whole thing is formalized with a contract."

"But we haven't even seen the contracts," Robin protested. "I'm not going to sign something I haven't read."

"I'll give them to you today," Reg replied. "Take them home and read them and let me know if there's anything you don't understand. After the showcase at the Supermarket I'm going to throw a party back here at the loft. We'll all sign then, in front of the press. That way we can take care of business and get a little extra publicity at the same time." He lit a cigarette and looked from Robin to Annette to Gail. "If any of you are unhappy with that arrangement, tell me now so I can find replacements right away."

"You mean, if we don't promise to sign the contracts, we're out of the band?" Annette asked.

"Business is business," he said with a shrug. "No contract, no band."

Robin glanced at the other girls. Annette shrugged. Gail was frowning and biting her fingernails. C.C. was smiling at Reg. "All right," Robin said slowly. "I guess that's fair."

Reg stood up and pushed his chair against the wall. "Oh, and one more thing. I've been trying to decide on a name for the band. Something exciting, dynamic. So far I've come up with Girl's Rock, Little Sisters, and C.C. and the Seniors. Now I thi—"

"But we already have a name!" Gail blurted out. "We're Overnight Sensation."

"Hmm," Reg said thoughtfully. "Cute. I'll think it over. So long, kids. See you tomorrow."

Robin stood up and walked to the window to get her coat. The Supermarket, she was thinking. Wow! She was so excited that she didn't even notice Matt standing in the doorway.

"Hi!" he said with a grin.

Startled, Robin looked up. "Oh! Oh, hi!"

Matt's hair was windblown and his cheeks were rosy. Drops of moisture covered his black wool coat and he was carrying a big red umbrella under his arm. "Just thought you might like to join me under my umbrella," he said. "It's starting to snow."

"Great! Come on in!"

As Robin turned to pick up her guitar case, she felt a hand on her shoulder. Turning, she found herself face to face with Reg. "Who's that?" he asked suspiciously.

Matt was inside the loft now, walking over to look at the instruments and equipment in the center of the room. "My boyfriend," Robin said. "Matt Stein."

"No visitors at rehearsals, Robin. That's a rule."

Robin frowned. "You never told us that. Besides, rehearsal's over."

"I'm telling you now. I don't want any outsiders hanging around. During the rest of the week you can do what you want, but inside this room I'm the boss."

Robin laughed humorlessly. "Dictator is more like it."

Reg didn't reply. Folding his arms across his chest, he just stood there, waiting for his order to be carried out. With a grunt of disgust Robin walked over to Matt and grabbed his arm. Startled, he looked up. "Let's go," she said impatiently, glancing back at Reg. "It's time to get out of here." Slipping her arm around his waist she half led, half dragged Matt past Reg and out the door.

"Hey, what's the big idea?" Matt asked angrily.

Robin didn't say anything until they were halfway down the stairs. "Reg makes me so mad," she said at last. "He said we couldn't have visitors at rehearsals and you had to leave."

Matt stared at Robin. "And because of that you practically had to shove me out the door?"

"I'm sorry," Robin said earnestly. "I just didn't want to upset Reg."

"Oh, I see," Matt retorted. "It's okay to treat me like a piece of furniture, just as long as you don't offend his royal highness."

Robin pushed open the downstairs door and walked out onto the sidewalk. The sky was filled with huge white snowflakes and the street was already turning white. Robin rested her guitar case against the steps and turned to face Matt. "Look, if it wasn't for Reg, this band wouldn't even exist," she said. "He bought our equipment, he rents the loft, he even booked the Supermarket for us to perform in."

"The Supermarket? You mean that rock club in the East Village?"

"That's right. We're playing there on December tenth."

"December tenth?" Matt cried, hitting his thigh with his fist. "Robin, that's the opening night of *Manhattan Magic!*"

Robin felt as if a lead weight had just dropped through her stomach. "Oh, Matt," she moaned, "this is awful!" Miserably she looked up at the falling snow and tried to think. "Maybe I could find someone to sit in for me opening night," she muttered, more to herself than to Matt. "I could put up some signs around campus, I guess." She looked at Matt and tried a tentative smile. "I'll find a replacement. And I'll still be there for the rest of the performances."

But Matt wasn't smiling. "Ever since you joined this band you've had no interest in anything else. All your time is spent practicing. Even when we're together, you talk nonstop about the band. Now you tell me you can't even come to the opening night of the play. I think that sucks!"

"But, Matt," Robin insisted, "I'll be there for all the other performances."

"That isn't the point." Angrily Matt grabbed Robin's arm and looked into her eyes. "To you this play is just an annoying little commitment you have to duck out of. But to me it's a whole lot more than that. It's my first play at NYU and my first starring role. It's just as special to me as that band is to you."

"Oh, Matt, I know the play is special. But this show at the Supermarket is more important than anything. Don't you understand? This is the band's first public performance. The place is going to be filled with music people. If we do well, we'll probably get a record contract—maybe even a TV show. How can I turn down a chance like that just because I promised to play my guitar in a college play?"

"I guess you can't," Matt said bitterly. "I guess anything that comes between you and your self-centered little dream of stardom has to be eliminated. And that includes our relationship."

Robin looked into Matt's angry face. His dark hair was powdered with snow and his eyes were as cold and gray as the sky. "Matt," she said helplessly, "you knew all along I wanted to be a rock musician."

Matt's laugh was cold and brittle. "How could I help but know it? You never talk about anything else."

Before Robin could answer, the door opened and Annette, C.C., and Gail walked outside. "Hey!" C.C. exclaimed. "It's snowing!"

Startled, Robin looked up at the girls. "Oh . . . hi, there," she said, trying to sound normal. She looked back at Matt and smiled weakly.

"Go with your friends," he said evenly. "You don't need to worry about me *or* the play. I'll find somebody else to play the guitar. And while I'm at it, I'll find myself a new girlfriend too." With that Matt turned on his heels and jogged off through the snow.

"Hey, Robin," C.C. said, walking down the steps with Annette and Gail. "Is that your boyfriend?"

"Was," she replied, her voice trembling. "In the past tense."

Gail looked into Robin's red-rimmed eyes. "What happened?" she asked with concern.

"It's this damn band," Robin said bitterly. "It takes up so much time, I can't pay attention to anything—or anyone—else."

"Tell me about it," Annette said, shaking her head. "Last week I forgot my sister's birthday. My dad almost killed me."

Gail sighed. "I know what you mean. My piano lessons have been awful. If they get any worse my teacher is going to call my parents."

"So what happened, Robin?" C.C. asked her.

"My boyfriend's starring in a play at school. I'm in it too—playing my guitar in a restaurant scene." She paused dramatically. "Opening night is December tenth—the night we're performing at the Supermarket!"

"Poor Robin," Gail said sympathetically.

"This band is screwing up my life!" Robin said with disgust. "Sometimes I wonder why I ever joined in the first place."

"The same reason we all did," replied C.C. "You want to be a star."

"That's not why *I* joined," said Gail. "It was the music that got me. I found out I love rock 'n' roll."

"Yeah," Robin said, managing a half smile. "The music. . . ."

Annette put her arm around Robin's shoulder. "Listen," she said reassuringly, "I've got just the thing to cheer you up. I keep my drums at my high school. On weekends the janitors let me in to practice. We could go over there right now and play some of your songs. You could even teach us a new one. Whaddaya say?"

"I don't know," Robin answered with a sigh. "I'm really depressed. Besides, I'd have to go home and get my amp."

"No problem. You can plug your guitar into the auditorium's PA system." She gave Robin's arm a playful punch. "Come on. I bet it'll cheer you up."

Robin sighed. "Oh, okay. It's better than sitting around crying over Matt."

"You bet," agreed Annette. She grabbed Robin's elbow. "Come on, troops. Forward march!" Giggling, the girls linked arms and started off down the snowy sidewalk.

|||||||||||||||||||||||||||| **11**

Luckily the janitor on duty at Annette's high school let the girls in without any hassle. They ran eagerly down the empty halls and into the auditorium. Annette opened the storage closet and pulled out her drums. Gail rolled the piano near the stage and Robin turned on the PA system and plugged into the control board. C.C. sang into an old microphone normally used by the principal during school assemblies.

The sound was abysmal, but the girls didn't care. For once they didn't have to practice the songs Reg had picked for them. No one was there to criticize their playing or to remind them to smile and dance and look cute. All that mattered now was having fun, and that's what they did. First they ran through Robin's song "You Can't Stop Me Now" until they had it down perfectly. "That sounds great!" Annette exclaimed. "Now teach us some of your other songs."

"Okay. Here's one called 'Free to Be.'" Robin played hard, concentrating on the music and trying to forget about Matt. To her surprise it seemed to work. While she was playing, she felt pretty good. It was only between songs that Matt's angry words came back to haunt her. "I guess anything that comes between you and your self-centered little dream of stardom has to be eliminated," he'd said.

Matt was being sarcastic, but Robin couldn't help wondering if maybe he was right. So far every guy she'd ever cared about had resented her love of rock 'n' roll. Some of them had teased her, some had criticized her, some—like Matt—had even accepted her at first. But in the end Robin always had to choose. Rock 'n' roll or boys. No matter how hard she tried, it seemed she could never have both.

After an hour of playing Annette put down her drumsticks and stood up. "Let's cool it for a while," she said. "I'm beat."

"It's cold in here," Gail said, tucking her hands in her armpits. "My fingers are getting stiff."

"I know." Annette nodded. "They keep the heat way down on the weekends."

C.C. reached in the pocket of her red leather jacket and pulled out a paper bag. "I've got just the thing," she told them. Opening the bag she produced a pint of brandy. "Guaranteed to create sparks," she said with a grin.

"Where'd you get that?" asked Robin.

"I bought it. If you act nineteen, you get treated that way. Remember?" She took a seat in the first row of the auditorium. "I use it to loosen up my voice. It's great stuff."

The girls sat down next to C.C. The auditorium was as dark and silent as a church. On the stage a single row of lights illuminated Annette's drums. C.C. opened the brandy bottle and took a swig of the brown liquid. It tingled on the way down and left a warm glow in her stomach. With a satisfied sigh she passed the bottle to Annette.

"You think you and your boyfriend will get back together?" C.C. asked, looking down the aisle at Robin.

"I doubt it," she answered with a sigh. "I guess I'm going to have to choose. Love or music. You can't have both."

Annette sniffed the brandy, then held her nose and took a gulp. "Yuck!" She passed the bottle to Gail and slouched in her seat. "Boys just hold you back," she said seriously. "They're okay as friends, but that's it."

Hesitantly Gail raised the bottle to her lips. When the brandy touched her tongue, the bitter taste made her gag. Coughing, she passed the bottle on to Robin. "Have you ever had a boyfriend?" she asked Annette.

"Naw. I'm friends with the guys in the jazz band, and in orchestra I hang out with the other drummers. To them I'm just one of the guys." She paused and cracked her gum. "That's the way I like it."

"You can have both love and music if you want it," C.C. said knowledgeably. "You just have to look for them in the same place." She was thinking of Reg, but suddenly she remembered how good it had felt to be in Kurt's arms, dancing across the patio to the soft strains of "My Funny Valentine." Could she have both love and music with someone like him? she wondered.

"You mean like you and Reg?" asked Annette.

"Of course," she answered quickly, pushing Kurt out of her mind. "Why not? Reg isn't going to hold me back, that's for sure. In fact, the better he likes me, the farther I'll go."

"You should move to Hollywood," muttered Robin. "The producers out there would just love to get you on their casting couches."

C.C. leaned forward and shot Robin a dirty look. "What do *you* know? Besides, I don't hang around with Reg just because he's running the band. We really like each other."

"I had a boyfriend once," Gail said softly. "We took piano lessons from the same teacher. His lesson was right after mine. We didn't go out or anything, but he used to call me up and talk about music. It was nice."

"Do you still see him?" Robin asked.

"No. We moved away and I started with a new teacher. His name is Mr. Dawson." She smiled dreamily. "He's fantastic!"

"Sounds like a serious crush to me," C.C. said with a chuckle.

"Oh, no," Gail protested. "I don't think of Mr. Dawson like *that*. He's a wonderful pianist, that's all."

Annette and C.C. looked at each other and smiled. "Sort of a spiritual relationship, huh, Gail?" C.C. teased.

Robin took a sip of the brandy and passed the bottle to Gail. "Don't let them get to you," she said. "I understand." She rested her head on the back of the seat. "I'm not cold anymore."

"What'd I tell you?" C.C. said with a nod. She reached over and took the bottle from Gail. "So listen, are you three going to sign the contracts?"

Annette leaned forward and rested her elbows on her knees. "I don't know what to do. If we sign with Reg, we have to go along with what he says. That means singing all those lightweight sixties songs and being advertised as a junior version of the Go-Go's."

"Yeah," agreed Robin. "I want to be a rock musician, not some rock producer's idea of the girl next door."

"But if you don't sign, you'll be out of the band," C.C. reminded them. But not me, she told herself. I already signed. I couldn't leave even if I wanted to. The thought made C.C. uncomfortable. If the girls leave the band, I'll be the only one left. Reg will bring in a bunch of new girls I don't even know, and I'll probably never see Annette or Robin or Gail again. "Come on," she urged the others, "how can you turn down a chance to perform at the Supermarket?"

Robin sighed. Half closing her eyes she tried to imagine that the dimly lit auditorium was the Supermarket and she was up onstage, strumming and singing. As she tore into a really hot guitar solo, the crowd went wild. Running to the edge of the stage, she dropped to one knee and looked out at the audience. The place was filled with gorgeous boys, all trying to reach up and touch her. Near the back she could just make out Matt, shouting and holding up a hand-lettered sign. I WAS WRONG, it said. PLEASE TAKE ME BACK!

Annette's voice brought Robin back to reality. "Look at what a good time we had playing Robin's songs just now. We weren't thinking about smiling or dancing or looking cute. We were really rocking."

"That's right," Gail agreed. "When we play Robin's songs we're Overnight Sensation. Not Girl's Rock or Little Sisters or—"

"—C.C. and the Seniors," C.C. said with a grin.

"Let's face it," Robin told them, "we're being packaged like a box of cereal. Still, how can we say no to a gig at the Supermarket? On our own it would take years to get booked there—if we ever did."

"So you're going to sign the contract?" C.C. asked eagerly. She pictured how pleased Reg would be when she told him. In fact, maybe she'd go over to his apartment and tell him later tonight.

Robin shrugged. "I guess so."

"Great!" exclaimed C.C. Yes, she told herself, I'll definitely go over tonight. "What about you, Annette?"

She sighed and took a sip of the brandy. "Probably."

"Gail?"

Gail swallowed hard. "I—I just don't know. I want to, but—" Her voice cracked. "I'm so confused!"

"Relax," Robin said gently. "You've still got time to decide. Talk it over with your parents."

Gail didn't answer. So many times she'd wanted to tell the girls the truth. My parents don't know I'm in the band, she imagined herself saying. They think I'm going to chamber music rehearsals.

Why can't I just say it? she wondered. But deep inside Gail knew the answer. She was just too embarrassed. To her the other girls seemed so grownup, so sophisticated and independent. She was sure they'd laugh at her if they knew how scared she was to stand up to her parents.

Gail looked up when she heard Annette giggling. "Hey, my gum tastes like brandy!"

"You and your gum!" C.C. said with a laugh. "How about sharing some with us for a change?"

"Sure." She pulled a pack from the pocket of her flannel shirt. After passing it out she lifted the brandy bottle. "Everybody take a sip." The girls did as they were told. "See?" she said triumphantly. "Brandy gum!"

"Maybe we can market it," suggested Robin. She put on a fake smile and spoke in the vapid tones of a TV announcer.

"Chew like a rock star! Buy Overnight Sensation brandy-flavored gum."

C.C. giggled. "The only gum with a kick as strong as Annette's bass drum!"

Robin sat back in her chair and laughed. "Well," she said
with a wry smile, "if we're going to sell out, we may as well
have fun doing it." Chewing her brandy-flavored gum she slid
down in the chair and closed her eyes. She felt warm and re-
laxed and a little high. So I lost my boyfriend, she thought
carelessly. So Reg won't let me play my songs. Who cares? I'm
going to be a rock star and that's all that counts.

"Can we come here anytime we want?" Gail asked her. "I
mean, will the janitors let us in?"

"Sure. I'll check with my band director, but it should be
okay."

Robin opened her eyes and sat up. "Then we could do this
every week," she said enthusiastically.

"Do what?" C.C. asked.

"Practice without Reg."

"Yeah," agreed Annette, hopping up on the stage. "We can
learn all your songs." She grabbed her drumsticks and hit a
drum roll. "Introducing the *real* Overnight Sensation. No
wimpy bubblegum songs. Just pure, unadulterated rock 'n'
roll!"

"Wait a minute," C.C. said nervously. "I don't think Reg is
going to like this. Maybe we should just—"

"Relax, C.C.," Annette told her. "You like to sing Robin's
songs, don't you?"

"Well, sure, but—"

"Then forget about Reg. What we do here is for us. Not
Little Sisters, not C.C. and the Seniors, just Overnight Sensation. Okay?"

"I—I guess so. . . ."

"Then come on!" Annette cried, motioning the girls up onto
the stage. Gail ran over to the piano, Robin strapped on her
guitar, and C.C. stood behind the microphone. "Okay, gang!"

Annette instructed. "Let's play Robin's song 'Free to Be.' One, two . . . one, two, three, four—"

Ignoring the feedback that shrieked through the PA system, the girls tore into the opening of the song. C.C. didn't know the words yet, so Robin ran up to the microphone to help her out. "I wanna be free, free to be all the things I want to be," she sang.

Everyone joined in on the next line. "You can't know what you want until you've tried everything, so come on, pretty baby, let me hear you sing." Putting Reg out of her mind C.C. grabbed the microphone and shouted out the chorus, "FREE TO BE!"

‖‖‖‖‖‖‖‖‖‖‖‖‖‖‖‖‖‖ **12**

The next month passed quickly. At first Robin tried to talk to Matt. She called his dorm a dozen times, but either he wasn't there or he wouldn't come to the phone. She looked for him around campus, but rarely saw him. When she did spot him, he always seemed to be out of reach—just getting on a bus, or hurrying into a classroom.

As the days turned into weeks, Robin felt more and more awkward. What did she want to say to Matt anyway? At this point she wasn't really sure. After all, it wasn't her fault the Supermarket gig turned out to be the same night as Matt's play, and she was damned if she was going to apologize. On the other hand she couldn't really expect Matt to apologize to *her*. She'd let him down and it was only natural for him to be mad.

Then one afternoon, just before Thanksgiving, Robin spotted Matt in Washington Square, walking arm and arm with his

Manhattan Magic costar. As she watched, the couple sat down on a snow-covered bench and started to kiss. Robin turned away, warm tears rolling down her wind-chilled cheeks. Well, she thought sadly, that's that. I'll just have to put Matt out of my mind.

But it wasn't easy to forget Matt's clear blue eyes, his deep laugh, or his soft, warm kisses. "Write a song about him," Annette suggested. "That'll get him out of your system." Robin agreed, and when the song was finished, she taught it to the girls. The only problem was, every time C.C. sang the chorus—"I'm still looking for those blue, blue eyes"—Robin got a lump in her throat and had to blink her eyes to hold back the tears. Even music, it seemed, couldn't take away the pain of losing Matt.

Meanwhile, Reg was driving the girls harder than ever. Rehearsals were longer and more frequent. Reg brought in a photographer to take publicity pictures and a choreographer to teach C.C. some dance moves. He worked out a song order for the concert that consisted of fifteen of the band's strongest performances. At the end of each rehearsal he went over the sort of questions they might be asked by reporters and coached them on their answers. Robin was strictly forbidden to compare the band to the Monkees, and Annette was warned never to use the words *exploitation* or *manipulation*. Everyone was reminded to be polite, smile a lot, and never, never curse.

Then there was the matter of the contracts. Robin took her copy home to her parents, who read it over and immediately showed it to their lawyer. Apparently the whole thing was legal, and typical of many management contracts. The rest of the weekend was spent talking about Robin's future. How important was the band to her? Did she realize she'd probably have to drop out of college if the group became successful? If the band flopped, would she promise to go back to school and get her degree? Finally, after two solid days of talking, the Quinns agreed that the choice was Robin's. If she wanted to sign the contract, she could. If not, that was okay too. The next day Robin told Reg she'd sign.

Annette hadn't talked to her parents about the contract at all. She knew her father wouldn't approve, but she didn't care. She was planning to leave home after graduation anyway. If the band succeeded, that would make it all the easier to move out. She, too, told Reg she would sign.

As for Gail, she still hadn't told her parents about the band, let alone the contract. When Reg asked her if she planned to sign, she didn't know what to say. If she refused, she'd have to quit the group. No more practices in the loft, plunking out funky chords on Reg's electric piano. No more jam sessions in the auditorium of Annette's high school. No more afternoons at Robin's house, listening to records and working out bass lines. The thought of giving up all that made Gail want to cry. The only solution was to convince her parents that playing in a rock 'n' roll band was all right. She didn't know how she'd do it, but she'd think of something. She just had to. "Okay," she told Reg. "I'll sign."

Meanwhile, despite their busy schedule, the girls were still getting together at Annette's high school to play Robin's songs and some other favorites that didn't fit in with the band's "image." The best thing about the private practices, said Robin, was that she could turn up the volume on her guitar and let it wail. "Reg always wants us to sound so tame," she complained to Annette. "You'd think we were playing lullabies instead of rock 'n' roll."

"Yeah," Annette agreed. "Besides, he never lets us play anything except love songs. What a bore!"

Gail loved the group's private practice sessions because she could let her creativity run wild. There was an endless number of ways to play every song, and she wanted to try them all. "In classical music you have to play what's written," she told Robin. "I never realized how much fun it is to jam."

Even C.C. agreed that the songs they played in private were more fun than the ones Reg picked. They were louder, wilder, and a lot sexier. C.C. loved to throw back her head and scream, and that was something you just couldn't do in a romantic little tune like "Chapel of Love."

Then finally, December tenth rolled around. The show wasn't until eight P.M., but Reg instructed the girls to come to the Supermarket at four o'clock for a sound check and run-through.

At noon on the day of the concert C.C. was driving through Short Hills with her mother. They were on their way to the Hillsbrook Country Club for a luncheon and meeting with the other girls who were coming out at the deb ball.

C.C. leaned against the window of the car and watched her mother. Mrs. Collins had bought a new dress and gotten her hair frosted for the occasion. She's dying to show up the other mothers, C.C. thought. She wants them to say, "Why, Diane, darling, you look smashing. Breaking up with Robert must agree with you!"

Despite Mrs. Collins's carefree manner, however, C.C. knew her mother was desperately trying to win her husband back. For one thing, she called his office at least twice a day. Usually he wouldn't talk to her, but she left dozens of messages, suggesting they get together "for old times' sake." Mrs. Collins didn't know where he was living now, so she couldn't call him at home, but C.C. noticed she spent a good deal of time in the city, frequenting his favorite stores and restaurants in the hope that she might "accidentally" run into him.

But not me, C.C. told herself firmly. I'm not running after him. If he doesn't care enough about me to show up for a lousy lunch date, then tough.

Still, part of her kept on hoping she'd see her father at least one more time. That was the main reason she was going through with the deb ball, even though she hated the whole idea. Her father was a big deal at the country club, and like C.C.'s mother, he put a lot of stock in doing the right thing. How would it look if he didn't show up for his own daughter's coming-out party? Besides, C.C. told herself, he loves me. I know he does. He won't let me down.

Mrs. Collins pulled the Jaguar into the parking lot of the Hillsbrook Country Club and turned off the engine. Peering into the rearview mirror, she patted her hair into place and checked her makeup. "What's this meeting about, anyway?" C.C. asked as she watched.

"I told you last week," Mrs. Collins replied, applying a fresh coat of lipstick. "It's about the ball. The mothers felt it would be a good idea to discuss some of the important points of etiquette—the receiving line, the first dance, that sort of thing."

"Well, just remember, I have to be at the Supermarket by four o'clock."

"So you've told me at least a hundred times." Mrs. Collins glanced disapprovingly at her daughter. "Sometimes I think I should have sent you to college this year. I just hope you'll get tired of this band business soon and settle down."

C.C. smiled to herself. Her mother didn't know about Reg and his plans for the band. She didn't know C.C. had signed a contract. She had no idea that her daughter would soon be making albums, going on tour, maybe even moving to Hollywood to star in a TV series.

Pretty soon I'll be gone, C.C. told herself. No more country clubs, no more deb balls, no more listening to my mother droning on about "making a good impression" and "meeting the right kind of people." I'll be singing rock 'n' roll. Me and the band. Me and Reg.

"Whatever you do, don't mention anything about the band," Mrs. Collins warned as they walked into the country club. "I don't want anyone to know you're involved in that sort of thing."

"Don't worry, Mother," C.C. replied coolly. "I won't do anything to upset your friends."

But Mrs. Collins wasn't listening. She'd spotted Patty Hawthorne and her mother and headed off across the lobby, dragging C.C. along with her. "Gladys, Patty, how *are* you? C.C. had a lovely time at your party, Patty. Didn't you, dear?"

For once C.C. didn't have to lie. She really had enjoyed talking to Kurt and dancing with him out on the patio. "Yes," she answered politely.

C.C. and her mother followed the Hawthornes to one of the

banquet rooms. Inside, eight girls and their mothers were lined up at one end of a long table, waiting to sample the elegant smorgasbord. C.C. joined the end of the line and looked around at the other girls. She knew most of them from her years at the country club and the many parties and dinners her mother had encouraged her to attend. Some of them were the sisters of boys she had gone out with. All of them were attractive, wealthy, well dressed, and polite, and all of them bored C.C. to death.

At the end of the food table an open bar was offering cocktails and wine. C.C. longed for a stiff shot of whiskey, but Mrs. Hawthorne handed her a small glass of wine instead. As she gulped it down, Mitzi Searles, one of C.C.'s former classmates at the Belmont School for Girls, came over. "So tell me," she whispered conspiratorially, "who's escorting you to the ball?"

C.C. thought about Kurt. Should she invite him? He would probably be more fun than any other "suitable" boy she could think of. But C.C. hadn't seen him since the night of Patty's birthday party, and she had no idea if he would accept her invitation. "I don't know," she told Mitzi. "Someone my mother chooses, I guess. How about you?"

"Well, I'm at Sarah Lawrence this year, you know, and believe me, I've met some absolute hunks!" She smiled with pleasure. "Too bad we can only have three escorts. I could easily find five or six!"

C.C. wondered how Mitzi would react if she found out one of her fellow debs was the lead singer in a rock band. While you're making time with some future stockbroker, she wanted to say, I'll be cutting my first album. But before she could give in to the impulse, Mrs. Collins appeared and led C.C. off to talk to someone else.

The lunch dragged on. C.C. gossiped with the other girls about their gowns, their escorts, and their plans for next year. Finally she asked someone the time. Two o'clock, and the run-through for the ball hadn't even begun!

I've got to get out of here, she thought impatiently. But how?

Mrs. Hawthorne clapped her hands. "Attention! Attention, everybody! The other mothers have asked me to talk a little bit about the ball and answer any questions you may have. Then we'll move into the ballroom and run through the introductions. After that, coffee and dessert will be served in the west lounge."

C.C. walked across the room to join her mother. "This is going to take forever," she whispered. "I have to leave."

"Don't worry, Catherine. We'll leave after the run-through. Just one cup of coffee and we'll go."

"But, Mother, you don't understand. I have to get to the East Village by four o'clock!"

Mrs. Collins frowned at her daughter. "I'm sure no one will care if you're a few minutes late. Being introduced to society is much more important to your future than a rock music band anyway. Someday you'll understand that and you'll thank me for insisting on this."

With an exasperated sigh C.C. turned away. As Mrs. Hawthorne prattled on, she looked out the window and wondered what Annette was doing right now. Oh, yeah, she was at her brother's confirmation party. Well, what about Gail? Reg? Robin? Suddenly C.C. had an idea. Leaving her empty wineglass on the table she turned back to her mother.

"Mother," she whispered urgently, "I have to go to the bathroom. I'll be right back."

Mrs. Collins gave her daughter a withering look. "Hurry up. And come right back."

C.C. walked quickly into the lobby and picked up the members' phone. First she dialed Reg, but all she got was his answering machine. Next she dialed the loft. No answer. She asked the operator for Gail's number, but when she called, Gail's brother said she wasn't home. There was no one left but Robin.

C.C. hesitated. She and Robin just didn't get along all that well. Briefly, she considered taking a taxi back to the city, but she didn't have enough money for such a long ride. She even thought about taking her mother's Jag, but she knew that would get her into even deeper trouble than her original plan.

Okay, then, C.C. told herself. I'll call Robin. After all, this is an emergency. An emergency that involves the band. She'll *have* to say yes.

C.C. dialed Robin's number. Hank answered. "Hold on," he said. "Robin, it's for you!"

Half a minute later Robin picked up the phone. "Hello?"

"Robin, this is C.C. I have a big favor to ask you. Can you get hold of a car?"

"Maybe. But why?"

"I'm in Short Hills, at the Hillsbrook Country Club. I don't have time to explain, but if you don't come out and get me right now, I won't make it to the Supermarket in time."

"Short Hills?" Robin repeated incredulously. "You want me to drive all the way out to Short Hills?"

"Please, Robin. You don't want me to miss the concert, do you?"

Robin sighed. "Hold on."

C.C. waited impatiently, drumming her fingers against the phone. She could hear Robin talking to someone, but she couldn't make out the words.

"C.C.?"

"Yes? Yes?"

"My mom's going to lend me the car. Just tell me how to get there."

"Oh, Robin, you're terrific!" C.C. hurried through the directions and hung up.

Back in the banquet room Mrs. Hawthorne was explaining the necessity of buying white gloves of the correct length. "They must come up to here," she said firmly, indicating the middle of her arm. "No more, no less." C.C. stood beside her mother and tried to look as if white gloves were the most interesting thing in the world.

After what seemed like hours, Mrs. Hawthorne led the girls down the hall and into the ballroom. The mothers stayed behind in the banquet room to have another cocktail and talk.

"The receiving line will form along the wall here," Mrs. Hawthorne told the girls. "Afterward, you'll have the first dance with your father."

The girls nodded eagerly. C.C. edged over to Mitzi Searles and asked the time. "Twenty of three," she whispered.

"Do me a favor, Mitzi," C.C. said conspiratorially. "Tell my mother I had to leave."

"What?" Mitzi looked shocked. "What do you mean?"

"She'll understand. I have to go now. Excuse me."

Before Mitzi could reply, C.C. slipped out of the ballroom and started down the hall. Apparently Mrs. Hawthorne hadn't noticed. She was telling the girls about the orchestra that had been hired for the ball. "The Stanley Winkleman Dance Band," she was saying. "They play something for everybody—even the kind of music you young people like."

C.C. was halfway down the hall when she saw a group of mothers walking out of the banquet room. Afraid her mother might be with them she ducked through the nearest door.

"Oh, my God!" she gasped, staring with horror at the row of urinals against the wall. "I'm in the men's room!"

Now what? she wondered, looking around. There was a window above the sink. Running across the room she climbed onto the edge of it and reached up to open the window. It slid open easily.

"Oh! Uh, excuse me," said a male voice behind her. "I think you've made a mistake."

C.C. froze. Should she turn around, or jump out the window and make a run for it? Before she could decide, two hands grabbed her from behind. "Hey! Let me go!" She spun around to face her captor. Kurt Vandenburg! "Kurt!" she cried. "What are you doing here?"

"The usual," he replied with a chuckle, releasing his hold on her waist. "A better question would be what are *you* doing here?"

"I'm leaving," she said, crouching precariously on the sink. "My band's playing at a club in the East Village tonight and I have to be there by four o'clock."

"Hey, that's great!" He paused and frowned. "But why don't you just walk out the front door?"

"It's a long story. Listen, I have to go. You won't tell anyone you saw me here, will you?"

Kurt laughed. "Your scandalous secret is safe with me." He leaned over and kissed her lightly on the lips. "A kiss for luck." He smiled. "Now, get out of here before someone else needs to use the john."

C.C. didn't move. Her lips still tingled from Kurt's kiss and her knees felt too weak to support her. Smiling dreamily, she gazed into his chocolate-brown eyes. Then, suddenly, the door to the men's room flew open and a middle-aged man walked in. With a burst of energy, C.C. stood on the sink and wriggled through the window. Luckily it was only a short drop to the ground.

Shivering in the December air, she jogged around to the front of the building just in time to see Robin pull into the parking lot. C.C. raised her arms in greeting and ran over to meet her.

"C.C.," Robin asked, rolling down her window, "what the hell is going on?"

"I'm staging a prison break," C.C. answered breathlessly. "Wait here while I get my other clothes." Running over to her mother's car she pulled her bag from the backseat. On the way back to Robin's orange Toyota she stopped to pull out her red leather jacket and put it on.

"I feel better already," she told Robin as they pulled out of the parking lot. "Thanks for coming."

Robin looked over at C.C. "Would you mind explaining what just happened?"

"You just helped me escape," she answered simply.

Robin laughed. "Escape from what?"

"The Land of the Preppies." C.C. shook her head until her long blond hair was a mass of wild tangles. Throwing her arm over the back of the seat she shot Robin a mischievous grin. "Onward, driver!" she said grandly. "It's time to rock!"

‖‖‖‖‖‖‖‖‖‖‖‖‖‖‖ **13**

Robin drove the car onto the entrance ramp to Route 78. "Maplewood isn't far from here, is it?" she asked, glancing over at C.C. "If we knew Gail's address, we could pick her up too."

"When we get to Maplewood, pull into a gas station and we can look it up in the phone book," C.C. suggested.

"Good thinking." She pointed to the glove compartment. "The map's in there. Take a look and tell me how to get there."

A few minutes later they turned onto Route 124 and headed into Maplewood. As they drove, C.C. told Robin about her upcoming deb ball.

"Boy," said Robin, "you sure don't seem like the deb type."

"I'm not," C.C. replied, kicking off her shoes. "It's all my parents' idea. They're really into that stuff." She took off her red leather jacket and pulled her dress up over her head.

"Hey!" cried Robin. "What are you doing?"

"Getting changed. I can't let Reg see me like this." She grabbed a pair of black leather pants and a glittery turquoise blouse from her bag and slipped them on.

Robin looked at C.C. "You really like Reg, don't you?" she asked.

C.C. pulled on a pair of turquoise high-heeled boots. "Sure I do," she said automatically, but when she tried to think about Reg, all she could see was Kurt's face. He'd kissed her so lightly their lips had barely touched, and yet C.C. felt hot all over just thinking about it.

"Do you see him a lot? Outside of the band, I mean."

"Who?" C.C. asked, still dreaming about Kurt.

Robin looked puzzled. "Reg, of course."

"Oh." C.C. looked out the window and sighed. Sure, she saw Reg a lot, but their relationship hadn't turned out quite the way she'd imagined. She'd figured that after they got to know each other, he would start taking her to rock parties and introducing her to his friends. Instead the only place Reg ever took her was back to his apartment.

Why do I keep going? C.C. asked herself. I never really want to, but then Reg kisses me and promises he'll take me to a party at Yoko Ono's house next weekend or a Billy Idol press conference next month, and somehow I always end up saying yes.

C.C. sighed. Whenever she walked into Reg's apartment and looked at his couch, her heart started pounding and her palms got damp with sweat. The more nervous she felt, the more whiskey she drank, until pretty soon she was too drunk to care. After that, well, one thing just led to another. . . .

Robin's voice brought C.C. back to the present. "I guess it's none of my business," she said. "Forget I asked."

Only then did C.C. realize she hadn't answered Robin's question. "Reg and I are really tight," she lied. "I just didn't want to say anything because I was afraid we'd get in a fight."

Robin smiled and shook her head. "I don't want to fight, especially not tonight."

"Me neither. And, Robin, thanks for picking me up. I really appreciate it."

"No problem." Robin turned off Milburn Avenue and drove through the center of Maplewood. At the first gas station, C.C. got out and looked up Gail's address in the phone book.

A few minutes later they pulled up in front of Gail's house. It was a modest white ranch house with yellow shutters and a yellow door. The girls hopped out of the car and walked across the lawn to the porch. Robin rang the bell.

An attractive middle-aged black woman answered the door. "Yes?" she asked.

"Hi," Robin said with a smile. "We're in the band with Gail. We thought she might like a ride, if she hasn't left already."

"The band?" Mrs. Harrison asked uncertainly. "What band?"

Robin opened her mouth to answer, but before she could make a sound, Gail appeared behind her mother, a look of horror on her usually calm face. "They mean the chamber-music group, Mom," she said loudly. "Hi, Robin, hi, C.C.," she added, staring meaningfully at her friends.

"Well, come in," Mrs. Harrison told them. "Do you two go to Juilliard?"

Robin and C.C. exchanged an uncertain glance. "Uh, yes," C.C. replied, hoping she'd picked the correct answer. She followed Robin into the house and looked around. The living room was simple and undistinguished except for the piano in the corner. Gail's father was standing behind a music stand, a violin in one hand and a bow in the other.

"These girls are in Gail's chamber-music group," Mrs. Harrison told him.

Mr. Harrison took a long look at C.C.'s turquoise boots, black leather pants, and red jacket. Slowly he turned his head to take in Robin's black jeans, black T-shirt, and denim jacket with the Elvis Costello pin on the pocket. "I see," he said doubtfully. "Well, when's this recital we keep hearing so much about?"

"They don't know," Gail said quickly.

"Maybe next month," Robin added with a weak smile.

"What instruments do you girls play?" Mrs. Harrison asked.

"Uh, I sing," C.C. told her.

"Clarinet," said Robin, naming the first orchestral instrument she could think of.

"Clarinet?" Mr. Harrison asked suspiciously. "Gail, I thought you said you were doing Schubert's *Trout Quintet*. There's no clarinet in that."

"I know," Gail answered quickly. "The clarinet's in the other piece. A Mozart clarinet quintet." She ran to the closet and grabbed her coat. "Come on, girls. Let's go."

Mr. Harrison stepped out from behind the music stand and

looked at his wife. "I'm going to call Mr. Dawson and find out what's really going on with this chamber-music group."

"Good idea."

"But, Daddy," Gail cried, "you don't have to—"

"No arguments, Gail," her father said firmly. "I've made up my mind."

Gail sighed. "Bye, Mom. Bye, Daddy," she said weakly. "See you later."

"Good-bye," Mr. Harrison answered seriously. "And, Gail, you've been staying out much too late. I want you home by nine tonight. Understand?"

Gail swallowed hard. "Yes, Daddy. Good-bye." Buttoning up her jacket, she followed Robin and C.C. out the door.

In the car C.C. turned to Gail. "What a weird scene! What was all that talk about Juilliard and a chamber-music group? I didn't know what to say."

Gail was in the backseat, slumped against the window. She tried to answer, but all that came out was a choked sob.

Robin started the car and drove away. "You never told your parents about the band, did you?" she asked gently.

"No," Gail whimpered. She wiped a tear from the corner of her eye. "Oh, Lord, what am I going to do?"

"Just tell them the truth," advised C.C. "So they get a little pissed off. Big deal. What can they do?"

"You don't understand," Gail moaned. "My parents have worked for years to give us the things they never had. I can't let them down."

"But how are you letting them down?" asked Robin. "Joining a rock band isn't so terrible."

"To them it is. They want me to make something of myself. And that means getting into Juilliard and becoming a concert pianist, not playing electric piano in a rock 'n' roll band."

"Poor Gail," Robin murmured. "I'm really sorry we showed up at your house. We sure didn't mean to get you into trouble."

"Relax," C.C. told her. "When your parents find out how famous you're going to be, they'll change their tune. Besides, think of all the money you'll be making. By the time we're through, you'll be able to *buy* a diploma from Juilliard!"

But Gail wasn't listening. She pulled a tissue from her coat pocket and blew her nose. "I'm supposed to be home at nine o'clock." She laughed hopelessly. "The show won't even be over by then."

"Don't worry," Robin told her. "We'll think of something." She glanced at the dashboard clock. Three forty-five. Cutting into the left lane she shifted into fourth and headed for the Holland Tunnel.

While Robin, C.C., and Gail were riding around New Jersey, Annette was at home in the middle of her brother Louis's confirmation party. Her grandparents, her aunts and uncles, her twelve cousins, and ten other family friends were there, too, eating, drinking, talking, and laughing. The entire dining-room table was covered with food and the refrigerator was filled with wine and beer. Cigarette and cigar smoke hung like smog over the noisy crowd. In the middle of it all sat Louis, grinning shyly and opening his presents.

Annette was standing in the corner of the dining room, nibbling on a piece of cake and talking to her uncle Mario. In honor of Louis's confirmation she was wearing her best clothes —a purple-and-black-striped dress with padded shoulders, and black high heels.

Glancing over her uncle's shoulder she noticed her father watching her from across the room. He'd been drinking steadily all afternoon, and with each beer his voice had gotten louder and more belligerent. So far she'd managed to stay away from him. Now, however, he walked straight toward her, limping slightly on his injured leg.

"Well," he said loudly, "if it isn't my darling daughter." He glanced at Mario. "She almost looks like a girl today, doesn't she?"

Blushing with embarrassment, Annette started to step around her father, but he put out his hand and grabbed her arm. "You've been avoiding me all day. Now you can stay put and talk to me."

"I have to change. I'm supposed to be in Manhattan by four."

"Oh, I forgot," Mr. Giraldi said sarcastically. "My daughter is a drummer in a big-time rock 'n' roll band." He looked at Mario. "She spends all her time in the city with her new friends. I guess we're not good enough for her."

"Knock it off," Annette muttered, pulling her arm out of her father's grasp.

"Hold on, young lady!" A few guests looked up from their conversations to see who was shouting. "Who said you could walk out on your brother's confirmation party?" Mr. Giraldi demanded. "This is a family affair, and like it or not, you're a member of this family."

Trying hard to stay calm, Annette looked into her father's eyes and spoke softly and slowly. "Dad, I've been here for three hours. Please let me go. I told you about this concert weeks ago."

"I don't remember any such thing." He put his arm around Annette's shoulders. "I want to talk to you. Look at Amy." He pointed to Annette's five-year-old sister. She was sitting on her grandfather's lap, hugging her doll and sipping soda from a Dixie cup. In her frilly pink dress and black patent leather shoes, she was the kind of little girl whom old ladies called "a perfect angel."

"You don't see *her* acting like a boy, do you?" Mr. Giraldi demanded. "She's a little girl and she likes it that way."

No longer able to control her anger Annette pulled away from her father and spun to face him. "She's like that because you force her to be that way. You tried it on me, but I wouldn't knuckle under. I'm an individual." She shook her head. "But you can't stand that, can you? You wanna bully everybody around and it pisses you off that you can't bully me!"

By now conversation had stopped and everyone in the dining room was staring at Annette and her father. Mrs. Giraldi had heard the shouting and come running in from the living room.

She was standing in the doorway, one hand held near her face, the other dangling helplessly at her side.

"You've got a hell of a nerve talking to me like that!" Mr. Giraldi said menacingly.

Annette knew she should keep quiet, but she couldn't help herself. All the anger she'd felt over the last few months came spilling out like lava from a volcano. "I'll tell you something else," she cried, pointing a finger at her father. "Ever since you got shot you've been moping around the house feeling sorry for yourself. Can't you see you're running Mom ragged?" She looked at her father with disgust. "You want me to look up to you and treat you like a hero. But how can I respect you when all you do is pick on me and put me down?" Annette's voice dropped to a whisper and hot tears stung her eyes. "Dad, it really hurts." Turning from her father, she pushed her way through the crowd of stunned relatives and friends.

"Annette, get back here!" her father called. He lurched drunkenly across the room and tried to grab her. But Annette was too fast for him. She dodged her way through the crowd and made it to the front door by the time her father reached the living room.

"Lou," Mrs. Giraldi said softly, reaching for her husband's arm. "Lou, let her go." Mr. Giraldi cursed under his breath, but stayed where he was.

Annette opened the front door and looked back over her shoulder. The crowded living room was silent. All eyes were on her. Ignoring their stares, Annette turned to face her father. Now was her chance to really tell him off, once and for all.

But looking at him standing there, leaning limply against the wall with his injured leg twisted behind him, all Annette's anger seemed to fade away and she was left with nothing but an aching sadness. What's the point of yelling at him? she asked herself. He doesn't understand me and he never will.

It was a depressing thought, but at the same time Annette felt relieved. I'm never going to please him, she told herself, so I might as well forget about it and just concentrate on pleasing myself. That's all I can do—that, and try to love him.

Wiping a tear from the corner of her eye, she squared her shoulders and took a deep breath. "Listen, everybody," she announced proudly. "My band is playing at the Supermarket tonight. Eight o'clock. You're all welcome to come."

She looked at her parents' stunned faces and smiled gently. "Good night, Mom. Good night, Dad. I love you both." Without waiting for a reply she turned and walked out the door.

|||||||||||||||||||||||||||| **14**

It was twenty past four when Robin finally found a parking space near the Supermarket. Leaping out of the car, the girls ran up and knocked on the front door. No answer. "Let's try the back," Robin suggested, leading them down a narrow alley that bordered the building. When they came to a blank brown door, all three girls pounded on it with their fists.

Instantly the door flew open and Annette peered out at them. "Where the hell have you been?" she demanded, pulling them inside. "Reg's about ready to lose it. He's been yelling his head off, acting like it's all my fault you're not here. Finally I told him you probably just forgot that the gig was tonight." She grinned. "I thought he was gonna throw a microphone at me!"

"I've been riding all over New Jersey, picking up C.C. and Gail," Robin explained as they walked inside. "It's a long story." She stared at Annette's dress. "What's with the fancy clothes?"

"Another long story. I made a hasty exit from my brother's confirmation party." She shrugged. "Reg says he has some clothes for me to wear."

Just then Reg appeared at the end of the corridor. "Nice of

you to show up," he said sarcastically. He was wearing a for-ties-style sport jacket with padded shoulders, and a thin red tie.

C.C. thought he looked breathtakingly handsome. "I'm sorry, Reg," she began. "We had to—"

"I don't want to hear it. Just get in here. We've got a lot of work to do."

The girls followed Reg along the corridor and into a tiny dressing room. Inside, an effeminate man with tousled blond hair sat in front of a mirror, filing his fingernails. When Reg entered, he jumped up.

"Okay, Terry, here they are," Reg told him. "Do your stuff."

"What's going on?" Robin asked. "Are you going to put makeup on us?"

"That's right, sweetie. I'm going to style your hair too." He walked behind her and ran his hands through her curly brown hair. "Hmm, this is going to be a challenge. Reggie, you want to go for a soft, wispy look, right?"

"That's right," Reg replied. "Something youthful and cute. Nothing too severe."

"Wait a minute," Robin said, pulling away. "I don't want anyone messing with my hair. I like it just the way it is."

"Yeah," agreed Annette. "We're rock musicians, you know, not finalists in the Miss Teenage America pageant."

"Relax, girls," Reg said reassuringly. "We're just going to add a little glamor."

"Well," Robin said skeptically, "I don't know. . . ."

"Go on, Terry," Reg ordered. "Get to work."

Terry sprayed Robin's hair with water and began brushing it out, using a blow dryer to relax her curls into a mane of loose, wispy waves. When he was satisfied, he coated the whole thing with hair spray.

Robin stared at herself in the mirror and frowned. "Yuck! I look like Farrah Fawcett."

"You're not making *my* hair like that," Annette said firmly.

"Oh, yes, we are," Reg answered. "That is, unless you don't want to go on tonight."

"Well?" Annette answered defiantly, standing up and facing

him. "What if I don't? The band can't play without a drummer, can it?"

"I've already thought of that," he told her calmly. "I brought along four young women who also happen to be studio musicians. If one of you decides not to go on, they'll just step in."

"What?" cried Robin. "That's not fair!"

Reg looked surprised. "Girls," he said earnestly, "I'm your manager and if you want this band to succeed, you're going to have to trust me. I'm doing all I can to make you famous, but if you won't cooperate . . ." He shrugged his shoulders. "Well, what can I do? Rock 'n' roll is a business, and in this band, I'm the boss."

Annette gave a snort of disgust and popped a stick of gum into her mouth. Crossing her arms across her chest she stared sullenly into the mirror.

"No gum onstage," Reg said, heading for the door. "Terry, send them down to me when you're finished," he added as he left.

C.C. frowned as Terry pulled her hair into a bouncy ponytail and tied it with a pink ribbon. "I don't know," she muttered. "It's cute, I guess, but . . . What do you think, Annette?"

Annette didn't answer. She just sat there and watched with horror as Terry fluffed up her hair and feathered her bangs. "Cripe!" she muttered when he was done. "I look like my head exploded!"

Terry walked over to Gail and gazed pensively down at her close-cropped Afro. "Hmm," he said, half to himself, "maybe if I use some gel . . ."

"Please," she begged him, her voice trembling, "don't do anything to my hair. If my parents see me—"

"Leave her alone!" Robin ordered. "She looks fine the way she is."

Terry looked thoughtful. "I guess you're right." He smiled and clapped his hands together. "Okay, sweeties, let's add some makeup."

When Terry was finished, the girls stared at themselves in the mirror. They looked fresh-faced and innocent, like models on the cover of *Seventeen*. "We can't play rock 'n' roll looking like this," Robin protested. "Haven't you ever seen Chrissie Hynde or Joan Jett? They wear tons of eyeliner and it looks great. Really hip and tough."

"I just do what I'm told," Terry said, ignoring the girls' complaints. "Now, come along, dears. Time to find Reggie."

Reg was standing backstage, talking to a heavily made-up woman in purple spandex pants and a pink T-shirt. When he saw the girls, he smiled cheerfully, just as if no unpleasant words had ever been exchanged. "Kids," he said enthusiastically, "you look great!"

Terry left and Reg threw his arm around the woman standing beside him. Wrinkles showed beneath her makeup, and her tight pants bulged at the hips. She had a camera slung over one shoulder and she was carrying a portable tape recorder.

"This is Marlene Pillsbury," Reg told the girls. "Marlene is a reporter for *Teen Trend* magazine. She'll be following you around this evening, asking questions and taking photos. I want you to cooperate with her completely."

"Hi, there," Marlene said, flipping on her tape recorder. She leaned over and spoke into the microphone. "I'm here backstage at the Supermarket with C.C. and the Seniors—"

"Hey!" cried Annette, "that's not our name!"

Marlene looked confused, but Reg turned to her and laughed reassuringly. "We were experimenting with a few different names," he told her. "I guess the girls just got confused." He glared at Annette. "Right?"

"Right," agreed C.C., glowing with pleasure. Reg *must* care for me, she thought happily. He's giving me top billing. "I'm C.C.," she told Marlene.

"No time for interviews now," Reg interrupted. "We're behind schedule and we've got to get the sound check out of the way. Come on, kids."

The girls followed Reg onstage. This is *it*, Robin thought, peering out into the empty club. In just a few hours the whole place is going to be packed with people, all waiting to hear what we can do. "I think I'm getting nervous." She gulped.

"I know what you mean," agreed Annette. "Up until now I was just numb. Then I saw the stage and my stomach turned over."

"Look at all those chairs," C.C. said, staring out over the footlights. "Do you think they'll all be filled?"

"How should I know?" Robin said sarcastically. "I'm just a member of the backup band. You're the big star, aren't you, C.C.?"

"Hey, I can't help it if Reg called the band C.C. and the Seniors," C.C. said defensively. "It wasn't *my* idea." Still, she told herself, those evenings in Reg's apartment certainly couldn't have hurt. . . .

"It doesn't matter," Gail told them. *"We* know we're Overnight Sensation, right?"

"Right!" they all agreed.

The girls spent the next hour running through their songs while Reg and the sound man adjusted the levels and replaced a malfunctioning microphone. Marlene Pillsbury looked on from the wings, occasionally stepping onstage to snap a picture. As usual Reg made the band sound soft and sweet, and he ignored Robin's complaint that she needed more volume on her guitar. "This is pop music," Reg growled, "not Blue Oyster Cult."

After the sound check Reg led the girls back to the dressing room so Terry could touch up their hair and makeup. While he worked, Marlene turned on her tape recorder and asked questions—what schools they went to, how they'd gotten into music, what they liked to do in their spare time, even what their favorite color was and where they bought their clothes.

"When can I get out of this dress?" Annette asked Reg. She'd already taken off her high heels.

"Right now," he replied, standing up. He glanced at Marlene. "I spent a lot of time coming up with an outfit that would convey C.C. and the Seniors' image. Young, energetic, fun-loving . . ." He smiled with satisfaction. "I think I found it." He opened a closet door and pulled out four black-and-white pleated miniskirts, four black blouses, and four pairs of white high-heeled boots with tassels. "What do you think?"

"Fantastic!" Marlene squealed. "They're so cute!"

"Hey," Robin said anxiously, "those look like cheerleader uniforms."

"They're supposed to." Reg held up one of the blouses. It was a short-sleeved cotton jersey with a V-neck. The letters C.C. had been sewn across the front in white. The other blouses said THE SENIORS.

"I'm not wearing any cheerleader outfit," Annette said loudly. "No way!"

Reg smiled, but his blue eyes were hard and cold. "Let's not argue in front of Marlene," he said quietly. He looked each girl in the eye. "And don't forget what I told you earlier. Any or all of you can be replaced." In a more cheerful voice he added, "Go on and get dressed. I'll meet you backstage in fifteen minutes. The place should be filling up by now and we don't want to keep them waiting." Reg stood up and walked to the door. "By the way," he added, "the music biz people will be sitting up front. Be sure to smile at them and make lots of eye contact. The rest of the audience will be the regular Saturday-night crowd. You girls are unknowns, so the place probably won't be packed. Still, this is a pretty popular place. We should have a fairly good turnout." He paused and looked at the girls. "You're going to be a hit tonight. Mark my words." Then he turned and walked out the door.

As soon as he'd left, the girls turned and looked at each other. "Chr-ist!" Robin began. "Can you believe—" Then she remembered Marlene was still there, taking pictures and taping every word they said. "Well," she stuttered, "I—I mean . . ."

"You girls don't look too happy," Marlene said eagerly, pointing her tape recorder at them. "Are you dissatisfied with the way Reg is managing you?"

Robin sighed. Yes! she wanted to scream. We're more than dissatisfied. We're fed up! Totally pissed off! M-A-D, *mad!* But if she spoke up, Marlene would get it all on tape. Then she'd go running to Reg and start asking him for his side of the story and the next thing Robin knew, she'd be out of the band.

For a long moment Robin considered letting that happen.

C.C. and the Seniors, she thought bitterly. God! We're being marketed as a quartet of mindless teenagers whose only desire is to jump around and look cute. Doesn't Reg realize that good rock 'n' roll is honest, powerful, even *dangerous* stuff? It's Bruce Springsteen singing about driving down the highway late at night, it's Chrissie Hynde warning the world to treat her right, it's the Clash, exposing the injustices of the system.

Still, Robin reminded herself, this is only the beginning of my career. So I have to compromise a little. It's no big deal. I'll just go along with Reg's plans until the band gets famous. Then, when my contract runs out, I can leave and go out on my own, playing my own songs and leading my own band.

Reassured—at least a little—Robin looked at Marlene and forced herself to smile. "We're satisfied with Reg," she said. "He knows what he's doing. Right, girls?"

Annette was grinding her gum. She looked up and shrugged. Gail cleared her throat, but said nothing. Only C.C. nodded enthusiastically. "Sure," she said. "He's the greatest."

Marlene's face fell. Obviously she'd been hoping for a juicy story. "I think I'll go talk to Reg," she told them. "See you in a few minutes." She snapped one final photograph and left.

"That woman gets on my nerves," Robin muttered as Marlene closed the door.

"Never mind that," Annette told her. "Why did you tell her we're satisfied with Reg? Look at us! He's turned us into a cross between The Monkees and the Dallas Cowboys Cheerleaders. It's disgusting!"

Robin threw up her arms in exasperation. "Listen, I'm as unhappy as you are. But what do you want me to do about it? We've come this far. I think we might as well get dressed and do the show. I mean, what have we got to lose?"

"Right," C.C. said enthusiastically. She had already put on her costume, and there was no denying she looked terrific. "Let's go out there and rock their socks off!"

The girls giggled. Smiling at each other, they felt a little better. For a moment no one spoke. Then Annette said, "I don't know about you guys, but I'm scared. What if we screw up?"

"We won't," replied C.C., but her voice sounded small and shaky.

"We're all nervous," Robin told them. "But just remember, we're in this together."

For once C.C. didn't argue. "We're going to be an Overnight Sensation," she said with a small smile. "Right?"

"Right!" Robin shouted, holding up a clenched fist. "Now, come on girls, let's go!"

||||||||||||||||||||||||| **15**

Decked out in their cheerleader costumes the girls left the dressing room and walked backstage. C.C. led the way, hips swaying. She wasn't crazy about her outfit, but as long as she had to wear it, she was going to do her best to look good. Behind her came Robin. She was sure her legs looked like beanpoles and she slouched in an effort to make her miniskirt cover her thighs. Gail followed, feeling shy and self-conscious in such a short skirt. Annette brought up the rear. Her outfit was a little too small for her and she was sure she looked fat and ugly. Miserably she cracked her gum and shuffled her boots along the floor.

Marlene Pillsbury was standing with Reg. As soon as the girls appeared, she began snapping pictures.

Reg put his arm around C.C.'s shoulder and she felt her heart thud against her ribs. "Remember, you're our focal point," he told her. "Don't let me down."

"I—I won't," she answered breathlessly.

"The place is packed," Reg continued, herding the girls toward the stage. "Annette," he added, handing her a tissue, "take out that gum." She rolled her eyes, but complied. "All right!" Reg cried. "Now get out there and knock 'em dead!"

Over the PA system a voice yelled, "Let's welcome C.C. and the Seniors!" Reg gave the girls a shove, and the next thing they knew, they were onstage. Brights lights shone in their eyes and beyond the glare they could just make out the audience—an endless sea of faces staring expectantly up at them. There was applause and a few cheers.

C.C.'s legs felt weak. She staggered to the microphone and tried to smile. A group of reporters, producers, and record-company types were spread out around the front tables. Light bulbs flashed as photos were taken. On the dance floor the regular Saturday-night crowd pushed forward, pointing and nudging each other.

"Uh-oh," someone shouted, "Go-Go's clones!"

"Who cares?" a voice answered. "They're cute!"

"Don't just stand there!" another voice yelled. "Play something!"

With a sinking feeling C.C. realized she was standing with her arms dangling at her sides, staring panic-stricken at the audience. Forcing herself to move, she held her hands poised over the keyboard of her Farfisa organ and shouted, "One, two, three, four—"

Behind her the girls broke into the bouncy introduction of "Girl's Rock." Robin's hands were trembling, but she stared at her guitar and concentrated on playing the right chords. Across the stage Gail plucked the bass strings and gazed openmouthed at the audience. She'd never even been to a rock club before, let alone performed at one, and she was mesmerized by the noisy, densely packed crowd of kids, all bouncing up and down in their seats or jumping around on the dance floor.

At the back of the stage Annette pounded away on the drums. Thank God I'm hidden back here, she thought gratefully. I'd die if anyone saw me in this outfit. Her stomach was full of butterflies and she wished she had a stick of gum.

When the chorus rolled around, the whole band joined in.

"When we get the urge, we have to converge, to make some sound and shake it around. That's girl's rock!"

C.C. looked down at the audience. No one was smiling. In fact, except for a few frowning faces, everyone looked pretty bored.

Maybe I'm not dancing around enough, C.C. worried. She pranced to the right, completely forgetting that the microphone stand was there. She hit it with her arm and it fell to the floor with a resounding crash. Unnerved, she leaned over to pick it up.

"Lean over a little farther!" someone in the audience shouted.

Fortunately a roadie ran onstage and righted the mike stand just as the song ended. There was a sprinkling of applause. "Rock and roll!" demanded a voice in the crowd.

But the next song was a slow one, "The Boy of My Dreams." The girls started playing and C.C. crooned the words, "He'll be so handsome, the boy of my dreams. . . ."

A few tough-looking boys with Stray Cats haircuts and leather jackets moved to the front of the dance floor. "Girls can't play rock 'n' roll!" one of them shouted.

"Yeah, this music is for wimps!" scoffed another.

"Turn around, baby!" they yelled. "Let's see what's under that little skirt!"

The girls had been nervous to begin with, but the rowdy crowd was making it even worse. Annette was losing the beat and Robin hit a couple of bad chords. Gail played all the right notes, but she was too nervous to look at the audience at all. C.C. was doing her best to keep things moving, but knocking over the microphone had embarrassed her so much, she'd stopped dancing for fear of doing it again.

The girls played on through three more songs—all covers of lightweight sixties tunes—but the crowd had started to drift away from the stage. A few people were dancing, but most of the audience was standing in the back or sitting at the tables, talking loudly.

Miserably Robin strummed the chords to "Chapel of Love." Reg really blew it when he booked us here, she told herself, surveying the kids in the audience. They had the latest haircuts and wore the latest clothes. Their T-shirts proclaimed the names of their favorite bands—critically acclaimed groups like X, R.E.M., and Talking Heads. This is a hip New York crowd, Robin thought angrily. They don't want to hear a bunch of silly teenyboppers. They like music with power, lyrics with a message, songs like . . . like *mine!*

Robin glanced backstage. Reg was standing in the wings with Marlene Pillsbury. His face was tense and pale. When he saw Robin looking at him, he yelled, "What's wrong with you girls? Dance around! Make eye contact with the big shots up front!"

"They hate us," Annette said in a loud stage whisper. "They look like a bunch of corpses out there."

If only we could play "You Can't Stop Me Now," Robin thought longingly. That would wake them up.

But the next song was "Do You Believe in Magic?" and when C.C. counted off the beat, Robin obediently played the opening chords.

Stepping up to the Farfisa organ, Gail closed her eyes and plunked out the chords. This was her special song, the one that made her the happiest. When the band played it, she could "believe in the magic that can set you free," and all her troubles seemed to disappear.

But tonight the magic just wasn't there. It's these ridiculous outfits, Gail told herself. We don't belong in matching costumes and we don't need fluffy hairstyles or makeup either. We're four different people, four *individuals.* That's what makes us special. That and Robin's songs.

Just then a gang of kids moved up to the front of the dance floor. There were at least a dozen of them and they all looked rowdy and more than a little high. "Rock 'n' roll!" came a drunken yell.

"Get the cheerleaders off the stage!" cried another.

"Where's your pom-poms?"

"At least the Go-Go's played their own songs!"

When the tune had ended, Robin stared into the crowd, her fists clenched in frustration. Why did I ever listen to Reg? she

asked herself angrily. All we're doing out here is making fools
of ourselves. No one realizes how good this band can really
sound. No one except us. "Damn!" she muttered furiously. "If
only we could play one of my songs!"

Annette was thinking the same thing. Instinctively she lifted
her sticks and softly beat out the drum part to "You Can't Stop
Me Now." Immediately Robin and Gail recognized what she
was playing. They turned to look at Annette, and when their
eyes met, Robin knew she couldn't keep quiet any longer. She
had to stop this charade and she had to stop it now. Before she
could chicken out, she ran up to the front of the stage and
grabbed the microphone out of C.C.'s hand. Startled, C.C.
stepped back. "What—?" she began, but Robin didn't bother to
answer.

"Listen, everybody!" she said loudly. "We're not C.C. and the
Seniors. That's just a name our manager thought up. This
band's called Overnight Sensation, and if you don't think we
know how to rock, just listen to this!"

With a whoop of joy Robin handed the mike back to C.C.
Running to the back of the stage, she turned up the volume and
treble on her amplifier and tore into the introduction of "You
Can't Stop Me Now." Annette and Gail came in a second later,
bashing out the bass line and the drumbeat with the force of a
hurricane. "Go on, C.C.!" Robin yelled over the music. "Sing!"

C.C. just stood there, wondering what to do. If she sang
Robin's song, Reg would be furious. If she didn't, she'd be left
there in the middle of the stage, doing nothing at all. Finally her
show-biz instincts prevailed. With knees shaking she raised the
microphone to her mouth and sang, "Well, I may be crazy but I
got this dream, I'm gonna make the whole world stand up and
scream. . . ."

The hecklers at the front of the audience had stopped yelling.
The crowd was quieting down and a few kids were moving up
toward the stage. With all eyes on her, C.C.'s confidence re-
turned. "I gotta find me a place where I belong," she sang
loudly. "So don't try to hold me down, cuz I'll be gone, gone,
gone!"

Triumphantly the other girls joined in on the chorus. "You can't stop me now! No, baby, you can't stop me now!"

Annette glanced offstage. Reg looked about ready to have a stroke. "What are you doing?" he cried. "The next song is supposed to be 'Chapel of Love.' Stop! Stop!" Annette just grinned and stopped hitting her high hat long enough to reach into her boot and pull out a stick of gum. Marlene Pillsbury snapped a photo of her popping it into her mouth.

C.C. looked out into the crowd. Everyone was watching her. With her head held high she pranced across the stage and belted out the next verse.

> *"Well, they told me to stay home and follow the rules,*
> *But I'm finished doing time in my neighborhood school.*
> *When graduation comes I'll be out on the street,*
> *Dancin' and singin' to a rock 'n' roll beat!"*

Robin ran up next to C.C. and sang into the microphone with her. "You can't stop me now! No, baby, you can't stop me now!"

When the song ended, the crowd let out a roar of approval. At the front tables the music people were talking and gesticulating wildly.

Without a pause Robin called out "Blue, Blue Eyes," and the girls started to play. For once the words didn't bring tears to Robin's eyes. She was too exhilarated to think about Matt now. When the time came for her guitar solo, she ran to the edge of the stage and dropped to one knee. Matt wasn't out there, holding up a sign that said PLEASE TAKE ME BACK! but she didn't care. She was onstage at the Supermarket, playing her song. That was enough.

After "Blue, Blue Eyes," the girls ran through five more of Robin's songs. Throughout the set the crowd's interest never waned. Some kids were standing up near the stage, bouncing along with the beat. Others were dancing near the back. As each song ended, they clapped and cheered and called for more. Even the music-business people joined in.

Finally Robin stepped up to the microphone and held up her

hands for silence. "This is our last song," she told the crowd. The kids moaned their disapproval, but Robin just smiled and continued. "Don't worry. You'll be hearing a lot more from us in the future. We're not called Overnight Sensation for nothing!" She turned to face the band. "Let's go, girls! One, two, three, four—"

Grinning and bouncing in place the girls tore into the introduction of "Free to Be." C.C. ran to the edge of the stage and looked into the crowd. By this time she had completely forgotten about Reg and how angry he must be. All she cared about was the audience. Their faces were turned up toward the stage and all eyes were gazing admiringly at her. With a satisfied smile she tossed her hair behind her shoulders and began to sing.

> *"I gotta be free, free to be,*
> *All the things that I want to be.*
> *Free to play my music and stay up all night,*
> *Free to see my baby's face in the morning light."*

The other girls joined in on the chorus.

> *"You can't know what you want until you've tried every-*
>   *thing,*
> *So come on, pretty baby, let me hear you sing,*
> *Free to be!"*

To C.C.'s delight the crowd joined in on the last line. By the end of the song everyone was shouting, "Free to be!" and raising their arms into the air. C.C. urged them on, dancing across the stage and pointing at the audience. Robin bounced and strummed behind her and even Gail swayed her hips as she plucked out her part on the bass.

The song ended with a crash of cymbals and the girls ran off the stage with the cheers of the crowd still ringing in their ears. They were greeted by a dozen reporters and photographers, all snapping pictures and calling out questions. Marlene Pillsbury was in front, thrusting her tape recorder in Robin's face.

To Robin's relief Reg was nowhere in sight. Ignoring the

reporters she wiped off her sweaty forehead with the back of her hand and turned to the other girls. "We did it!" she cried, her face glowing. "We played our own music and the crowd loved it!"

"Reg is going to kill us," C.C. moaned.

"Who cares?" laughed Annette. "We're an overnight sensation." She held her hand out so Gail could slap her five. "We don't need Reg anymore!"

############ **16**

A moment later Reg broke through the crowd and advanced toward the girls. To their amazement they saw that he was smiling. Throwing his arms around Robin and C.C., he turned to the reporters and said, "I know you're all wondering what happened out there. Well, I figured the best way to draw attention to the band was to do something really wild, really unusual. That's why I had the girls start off as C.C. and the Seniors, playing those bouncy bubblegum songs. I knew when they announced their real name and broke into a high-powered new tune, everyone would sit up and take notice." He chuckled with pleasure. "I guess it worked."

"You mean that whole thing was staged?" one of the reporters asked incredulously.

"Of course," Reg replied. "And that's the kind of thing you can expect from Overnight Sensation in the future as well. They're unpredictable, offbeat . . . unique!"

Robin could hardly believe her ears. How dare Reg claim the whole performance had been planned in advance! How *dare* he take all the credit! Impulsively Robin pushed Reg's arm off her shoulder and stepped forward. "That's a bunch of bull!" she cried indignantly. "Reg had nothing to do with the second part of our performance. He just wanted us to bounce around and smile and sing all those bubblegum songs."

Reg tried to laugh. "Yes, of course. I wanted the girls to *start* that way—"

"And stay that way too," Annette broke in. "Reg has nothing to do with Overnight Sensation. Gail thought up the name and Robin wrote all the songs. We've been practicing together in our spare time. Reg didn't know anything about it."

"That's right," agreed Gail. "If it had been up to Reg, we would have stayed C.C. and the Seniors forever. He tried to tell us what songs to play, what clothes to wear, how to style our hair—everything!"

The only girl who hadn't spoken up was C.C. Reg's arm was still around her shoulders, only now his fingers were digging painfully into her upper arm. For the time being, she decided, she'd better keep her mouth shut.

"What are you going to do now, girls?" one of the reporters asked.

"The publicity party is still on," Reg announced loudly. "The girls and I will be signing a management contract later this evening. Greene Street in SoHo. We'll be happy to answer your questions there." Reg grabbed Robin's arm and started to pull her away from the reporters. "Come on, girls," he said firmly.

But Robin dug her heels in and refused to budge. "I don't know about the other girls," she said boldly, "but I'm not signing anything. You can do what you want with C.C. and the Seniors, but you'll have to find a new guitar player. I quit!"

"Me too!" Annette told the crowd. "We're Overnight Sensation and we don't need any manipulative males telling us what to do."

"I agree," said Gail. Her voice was soft but decisive and her dark eyes burned with intensity. "I quit!"

Everyone turned to C.C. "What about you?" Marlene Pillsbury demanded. "Do you agree with the rest of the band?"

But before C.C. could answer, Reg spoke up. "C.C. is under

contract to me," he said smugly. "We signed an agreement over two months ago."

Robin groaned. "I'd forgotten about that!"

Reg shot Robin a self-satisfied smile. "The other girls can do what they want," he told the reporters, "but frankly, I don't think they'll get very far without C.C. I knew from the start she was the most talented of the bunch."

"Will you put together a new C.C. and the Seniors?" a reporter asked.

"I doubt it. I think C.C. deserves a better backup band than these amateurs can provide. I'm going to put together a new group of male musicians. And of course C.C. will sing lead."

Annette was fuming. "She will not! She's part of Overnight Sensation." She reached for C.C.'s hand. "Come on, let's get out of here."

Reg grabbed C.C.'s upper arm and held it tight. "The contract you signed gives me exclusive rights to manage and merchandize you," he said tersely. "If you perform anywhere with these girls, I'm going to have to take you to court."

C.C. swallowed hard. She loved singing Robin's songs. She loved hanging out with Annette and Gail and Robin, talking and laughing, sharing secrets and playing music. What they had together was special. How could she give all that up and start over with another band? "Reg—" she began.

"Think about it, C.C.," he said softly. "Your career would be over. Finished before it even began."

C.C. felt sick. Would Reg really do that to me? she wondered miserably. I thought I meant something to him. I thought he really cared.

"Come on, C.C.," Annette pleaded. "Overnight Sensation wouldn't be the same without you. Don't listen to Reg."

But what's the alternative? C.C. wondered. She had read about what had happened to Bruce Springsteen. His manager sued him and the judge decreed that he couldn't perform until the case was settled. When it was all over, Springsteen hadn't been onstage for over a year.

No, C.C. thought fearfully. I can't let that happen. Not now, when I'm so close to making it.

"I'm staying with Reg," she said sadly. "I—I have to."

"But, C.C.—" Gail began.

"Forget it," Robin said disdainfully. "If that's what she wants, let her. We'll find a new lead singer." She turned to the crowd of journalists and photographers. "Overnight Sensation will be back," she told them. "You haven't heard the end of us yet!" Linking arms with Annette and Gail, she started off down the corridor.

Annette hesitated. Looking over her shoulder she met C.C.'s eye. "I'll call you," she said gently. Then she turned and ran after Robin and Gail.

C.C. just stood there, watching the girls leave. Reporters were asking her questions, but she wasn't listening. How could she when she felt so upset, so miserable, so *confused?*

I should be happy, she told herself. Reg told everybody he thinks I'm the most talented of all the girls. He's going to put together a backup band just for me. I'm going to be a star, just like he promised.

But none of that seemed to matter now. All she could think about was Overnight Sensation. They were probably sitting in the dressing room right now, blaming C.C. for everything that had happened.

But it's not my fault things turned out like this, she told herself. If Robin hadn't taken over the concert, we'd still be together, same as before. I mean, things weren't so bad with Reg, were they? Maybe it wasn't so great singing teenybopper songs and wearing cheerleader outfits, but if it could make us famous, who cares? We could still get together and sing Robin's songs on the side.

But there was no chance of that now. The other girls had walked away and left her. Well, she told herself, if that's how they feel, then tough. Let them find a new lead singer. I'm going to be in a new band. I don't need them.

Slipping her arm around Reg's waist, she looked at the reporters and said smoothly, "I'm delighted to be working with

Reg. We're very close. And I'm sure our next band will be even better than C.C. and the Seniors. Right, Reg?"

"Absolutely." Reg looked at C.C. and smiled with satisfaction. "I think we make an excellent team."

Back in the dressing room Robin, Annette, and Gail were taking off their cheerleader costumes and putting on their own clothes. Annette threw her tasseled boots onto the floor and sighed. "Overnight Sensation won't be the same without C.C.," she said sadly.

Robin lifted her T-shirt over her head. "Forget C.C.," she said angrily. "She made her choice right from the beginning. Reg is a lot more important to her than we are."

"I don't know about that," Annette retorted. "If she really wanted to make Reg happy, she could have walked offstage the minute we started playing your songs. But she didn't, did she? She stayed and put on a great show."

Robin flopped down on one of the chairs and put her head in her hands. "Oh, man, I don't know. Maybe I should have just kept my mouth shut. If it wasn't for me, we'd probably all be signing a record contract right now." She ran her hands over her lacquered hair. "As it is, we've lost our manager *and* our lead singer."

"That's not all," Gail said glumly.

Robin and Annette looked at her. "What do you mean?" they both asked at once.

"By now my parents must know I haven't been going to chamber music rehearsals every afternoon." She let out a ragged sigh. "I can't be in the band anymore. They won't let me."

"But, Gail," Robin protested, "you can convince them. Tell them how much the band means to you. They'll understand."

"*My* parents don't approve of the band," Annette added, "but I'm in it anyway. Besides, I'm moving out after graduation. You should do the same thing."

Gail shook her head. "I can't. I'm applying to Juilliard. It's so expensive I'll have to win a scholarship and get a job *and* live at home just to afford it."

Annette shrugged. "What if you don't get in?"

"I have to!" Gail cried. "My parents have been working and planning all my life so I could go to Juilliard. I can't let them down."

Robin sighed. "Well, so much for Overnight Sensation," she said sadly. "It was a nice dream while it lasted."

"Hey," Annette protested, "we can't give up yet. We'll figure something out."

"Oh, no!" Gail moaned, looking down at her watch. "My father told me to be home by nine. It's after eleven now!"

"Come on," Robin told them. "I'll drive you both home."

Annette shook her head. "I'm not going home tonight. After what I said to my father, my ass is grass."

Robin sighed. "Well, then, you better stay over at my house. Come on."

Leaving their C.C. and the Seniors outfits lying in a pile on the floor, the girls left the dressing room and headed down the corridor to the exit. As they reached the door they heard footsteps pounding down the hall behind them.

"Hey, Robin!" a male voice called after them. "Hey, wait up!"

Turning, Robin saw a young man jogging toward her. As he got closer, Robin could see he had a long, attractive face with high cheekbones and dark eyes. His brown hair was cut short on the sides, but the top was loose and wavy. One lock, longer than the others, hung down over his forehead. He was wearing brown corduroy pants and a baggy black sweater and he had a camera around his neck that bounced against his chest as he ran.

"Robin?" he asked, breaking into a smile. "Can I talk to you a minute?"

"Are you a reporter?" Robin asked warily. If there was one thing she didn't want to do right now, it was answer a lot of questions about the band.

"I'm writing about the concert for *Rock Rag*," he told her. "It's a new magazine that covers the music scene in lower Manhattan."

"No interviews," Robin said tersely. "We're in a hurry." She turned to leave.

"Hey, hold on!" he cried indignantly. "Don't act so stuck up. You're not a rock star yet, you know." Robin opened her mouth to reply, but the boy kept right on talking. "Listen, I'm not looking for an interview. I just wanted to tell you I think it was great the way you stood up to Reg Barthwaite back there. You've got integrity. That's a rare thing in the music world these days."

"Uh, thanks," she muttered, blushing slightly.

"Your songs aren't half bad either," he continued. "If you keep at it, you're going to develop into a pretty good songwriter in a year or two."

"A year or two?" Annette retorted. "She's a terrific song-writer right now!"

The young man glanced at Annette and smiled indulgently. "Well, anyhow," he said, looking back at Robin, "I just wanted to give you my card. I've produced demo tapes and singles for a few local bands. When you're ready to make a tape, I might be interested."

He handed Robin a business card. IAN HARKIN, it read. GUI-TAR, KEYBOARDS, ARRANGING AND PRODUCING.

Robin looked up into Ian's impassive face and tried to reconcile her conflicting feelings. This guy certainly has a lot of nerve, she thought irritably. The way he comes on, you'd think he was Paul McCartney or something. On the other hand there was something about Ian that appealed to Robin. She liked his lanky body, his brown eyes, and his wild wavy hair. When he'd first smiled at her, his whole face had lit up like a Christmas tree. Robin wished she could make him smile like that again.

"Well," she said uncertainly, "if we ever need a producer, maybe I'll call you." She smiled grudgingly. "Thanks."

Ian smiled too. Not the five-hundred-watt smile he'd shown her before, but a nice smile all the same. Quiet and thoughtful and confident. Nice.

"Come on," Annette said impatiently. "Let's get out of here." She opened the door and stepped into the alley.

"Oh . . . right," Robin muttered, forcing herself to look away from Ian's face. "So long," she called over her shoulder.

"So long, Robin. See you soon, I hope."

Outside the night was cold and damp. A few stray snowflakes fluttered past the streetlights. The girls hurried down the alley and out onto St. Mark's Place. Some kids were milling around outside the club, smoking and talking, but most of the audience was still inside, dancing to the prerecorded music that would continue until three or four in the morning.

"Annette!" A small, dark-haired woman stepped out of the shadows.

Annette spun around and found herself face to face with her mother. "Mom!" she cried in amazement. "What are you doing here?"

Mrs. Giraldi came forward and hugged her eldest daughter. Looking up into her face, she frowned and asked, "What happened to your hair? You look like your head exploded!"

The girls burst out laughing and even Annette had to smile. "Mom," she said, "this is Robin Quinn and Gail Harrison. They're in the band with me."

Mrs. Giraldi smiled sweetly. "Hello, girls." She turned back to Annette. "Let's go home now, dear."

Annette stiffened. "No way," she said, shaking her head. "I can't face Dad. Besides, I know he doesn't want me there. Not tonight, not *ever.*"

"That's not true, dear. He loves you and he wants you to come home."

"Oh, sure," Annette said sarcastically. "What did he do? Send you here to bring me back? He probably wants me to come crawling home just so he can have the pleasure of personally throwing me out."

Mrs. Giraldi shook her head. "Your father didn't want me to come get you. In fact, he forbade me to leave the house. But I knew after what happened, you'd think you weren't welcome at home and, well, I couldn't bear that." She smiled shyly. "No matter how bad things get sometimes, we're still family, and family sticks together."

Annette stared open mouthed at her mother. In her entire life she had never once seen her mother stand up to her father. "You mean Dad told you to stay home, but you came here anyway?" she asked incredulously.

Mrs. Giraldi nodded. "I was scared to death," she said with a nervous giggle. "I mean, he's my *husband!*" She paused and took a deep breath. "But I know, deep down, he feels the same way I do. He may be angry now, but he'd never forgive himself if he felt he'd driven you away." She smiled self-consciously. "Besides, your father passed out on the sofa hours ago. He never even knew I left."

Annette gazed admiringly at her mother and shook her head. "Mom, you're too much!" She turned to Robin and smiled. "Thanks for inviting me to sleep over, but I guess I'll be going home after all."

"Great. I'll call you tomorrow."

"Better wait for me to call you," Annette told her. "My dad'll be on the warpath when he wakes up. It may take him a few years to calm down."

Robin chuckled. "Okay. Good night." Together she and Gail turned and headed off down the street.

When they were gone, Annette looked back at her mother. Mrs. Giraldi was gazing uncertainly up and down the street. "This doesn't look like a very nice neighborhood," she said with a worried frown. "Couldn't you find a place to play your music that's a little closer to home? Maybe in the basement of the church. I think they hold the CYO dances there."

Annette laughed and threw her arm around her mother's shoulder. "Come on, Mom," she said, giving her a gentle squeeze. "We can talk about all that later. Right now I just wanna go home."

|||||||||||||||||||||||| **17**

Robin called Gail the next day. Mr. Harrison answered the phone and told her in no uncertain terms that Gail was no longer in the band. "Gail is grounded," he said, "and she's not allowed to talk on the telephone either."

"Oh. Well, could you tell her—"

"No, I could not. And by the way, young lady, my daughter told me it was your guitar playing that first got her interested in rock 'n' roll. Well, if that's the case, I'm very sorry Gail ever met you, and I'll thank you to keep away from her from now on." Before Robin could speak a word in her own defense, Mr. Harrison hung up.

Robin was dying to call Annette, but remembering her friend's warning that her father would be "on the warpath," she refrained. One angry father a day was all she could handle, Robin decided. Instead she accepted a cup of hot chocolate from her mother and a sympathetic hug from her dad, and retreated to her room.

She was lying on her bed, plucking out a mournful blues tune on her guitar, when she heard the doorbell ring. A minute later her mother called, "Robin! There's someone here to see you!" With a sigh she put down her guitar and dragged herself to the living room.

When Robin saw who it was, she froze. Matt was standing in the foyer, nervously brushing a piece of lint off his gray corduroy pants. Automatically Robin's heart picked up speed. "Uh, hi, Matt," she said, trying to sound casual. "Come on in."

"Thanks." Matt took off his coat, and glanced into the living room, where Mr. and Mrs. Quinn were watching a talk show on television. "Robin, can I talk to you? Alone, I mean."

"Uh, sure," she said, avoiding his eyes. "Come on." Robin walked into her room, acutely aware that Matt was directly behind her. "Sit down," she said, indicating the chair next to her desk. Pushing her guitar aside, she sat stiffly on the edge of her bed.

Matt sat down and cleared his throat. A long moment passed. Finally he looked up and met Robin's eye. "I . . . well, I came to ask if you'd consider going out with me again."

Robin didn't know what to say. It had taken her weeks to forget about Matt. And now, when she'd finally succeeded— well, almost, anyway—here he was, wanting to get involved again. "I thought you were seeing someone else," she said, buying time.

"I was but, uh, it didn't work out."

Robin refused to offer any sympathy. Instead, she said, "You told me you didn't want to see me anymore. You said I was too wrapped up in rock 'n' roll to care about anything else."

"Yeah, well, I guess I was overreacting." He laughed uncomfortably. "Besides, I read in the paper that the band broke up, so I thought—"

"You what?" Robin broke in excitedly. "What newspaper? What did you read?"

"In *The Village Voice*. There's an article about how Reg Barthwaite tried to turn you into teen idols. It said that C.C. is under contract with Reg and he's putting her in a new band. I figured that meant you weren't in the group anymore."

"And if I'm not in the band, I'll have more time for you. Is that what you were thinking?"

"No! I mean, well . . ." Matt hesitated. "I guess I should be honest. When you joined the band, it looked as if you were going to get famous almost overnight. That's the way you talked, anyway, and it made me jealous. I know you want to play rock 'n' roll, and that's fine with me, but I just couldn't handle the idea of you becoming a big star while I was still acting in my first college play." He paused and smiled. "But now we're equal again. You can join a band at school and I can—"

"Matt," Robin said firmly, "it's over." Actually she hadn't realized it until she opened her mouth. In fact, the whole time Matt was speaking, she'd been thinking, *He wants me back! From now on everything is going to be just fine.* Then, suddenly, she'd told him the relationship was over, and as she heard the words, she knew they were true.

"But, Robin—" Matt began.

"Listen," she said, standing up and facing him, "it just won't work. Maybe I'm just not ready for a relationship. I'm not sure. All I know is right now I've got to put all my energy into my music. I don't have time to be wondering if I'm spending enough time with you or if I'm succeeding faster than you or if I'm making you jealous. That's pretty self-centered, I know, but that's just the way it is."

"Well, if that's the way you feel . . ." Matt said flatly. He sighed and stood up.

Robin could feel him moving farther away with each passing second and part of her longed to reach out and hug him and say, "I didn't mean it, Matt! I love you!" But she knew it wasn't true, so she took a deep breath and said, "That's the way I feel."

"Okay. Well, I guess I'd better leave. I've got a lot of work to do at the library." He stepped around Robin and opened the door. Robin started after him, but he looked over his shoulder and said, "Don't bother. I can let myself out."

"Bye, Matt," she said helplessly.

"So long. I'll see you around." He walked into the hall and closed the door behind him.

Turning from the door Robin threw herself on the bed and stared up at the ceiling. "He's gone," she whispered mournfully. But the funny thing was, she didn't feel all that bad. Dutifully she reached for her guitar and strummed a few chords from her song "Blue, Blue Eyes." But instead of thinking about Matt she found herself dreaming about another pair of eyes—

brown, deep-set eyes, with two little wrinkles in between. Ian Harkin!

Why am I thinking about him? Robin wondered. Sure, he's good looking—tall and slender with soft brown curls and a terrific smile. But he's stuck up too. Imagine telling me I'd be a pretty good songwriter *in a year or two*. Some nerve!

Robin stood up and walked to the bureau, where she'd left Ian's business card when she came home last night. She picked it up and read it over. Nice name, she conceded. Nice face. Well, if Overnight Sensation ever gets back together, maybe I'll call him up.

If. That was the key word. Robin put down the business card and sighed wearily. No band, no boyfriend. Things looked pretty grim.

After school on Monday, Annette called Robin. "Well, I'm still alive," she told her friend. "Let's meet in the Village after dinner."

"In the SoHo Saloon?"

Annette laughed, but her heart wasn't in it. "I'm more in the mood for ice cream," she said. "When I'm depressed, I pig out."

That evening the girls met at the Big Dipper, an ice cream shop near Robin's house. After brief hellos they found a table and ordered large sundaes with extra hot fudge. "So what happened when your dad woke up?" Robin asked.

"Well, I'd completely forgotten that today was my father's first day back at work. He's a cop, you know, and he got shot last year during a bank robbery. He's got a desk job now." Robin nodded. "Anyway, he woke up with a terrible hangover, but he had to be at work by eight. All he did was sit at the dining room table, drinking black coffee and holding his head. He didn't even look at me." Annette smiled. "To tell you the truth, I don't think he even remembers what I said to him. I hope not, anyway."

The waiter brought the sundaes and Robin took a bite of hers. "Sounds like you lucked out."

"No kidding! Anyway, my mom thinks things are going to be better now that he's back at work." She shrugged. "At least he won't be around as much." She licked some hot fudge off her spoon. "Did you talk to Gail?"

"Not exactly. I talked to her father, though, and he's got me pegged as a close personal friend of Satan." She sighed. "He says she's out of the band. She's grounded, too, and she can't even talk on the phone."

Annette nodded sadly. "I called C.C. last night."

"That's nice. I'm sure she and Reg had a wonderful time at the press party, telling all those reporters what losers we are."

"Come on. C.C.'s not like that. She'd rather be playing with us—she told me so. But what can she do? She signed the contract."

"True," Robin conceded. "You know, C.C. drove me nuts sometimes, but she sure could sing. It's hard to imagine Overnight Sensation without her."

Annette finished off her sundae and sighed. "Well, what happens now? Do we just forget about the band or what?"

"I don't know. I guess we could try to find two new members. . . ." Robin's voice trailed off and she looked up at Annette.

"Yeah," she answered uncertainly. "I guess we could. . . ."

Robin frowned and shook her head. "Annette, I really blew it. If I'd just kept my mouth shut and played the songs Reg told us to play, we'd be recording our first album now." She laughed ruefully. "What a moron! Thanks to me we lose out all around. No fame, no money . . . no band!"

"Robin," Annette said firmly, "cut the self-pity, okay? You heard what that reporter from *Rock Rag* told you. It took integrity to stand up to Reg. Integrity and guts."

"Maybe. But it would have taken more guts to just quit quietly before the concert even started. That way Reg could have sent in one of his studio musician friends to replace me, and the rest of you girls wouldn't have had to get involved."

"Wait a minute," Annette protested. "You make it sound like this was all your idea. You weren't forcing us to play your songs, you know. We *wanted* to." She pointed her finger at Robin for emphasis. "And I don't regret it either. Just seeing the look on Reg's face when we broke into 'You Can't Stop Me Now' made it all worthwhile." She laughed. "I thought he was going to croak!"

Robin giggled. "Well, at least we had one evening of stardom. That's more than most people get." She reached into her coat pocket and pulled out a crumpled copy of *The Village Voice*. "Have you seen this?"

"No," Annette answered eagerly. "Is it about us?"

"You bet. It's just a little article, and it's more about Reg than us, but still . . ." She opened the paper and started to read. " 'It's not easy to surprise a rock 'n' roll audience these days, but last night at the Supermarket, four teenage girls did just that. The band—' "

"Hold on," interrupted Annette, holding up her hand. "I can't concentrate when I'm hungry. Waiter!" she called, banging her spoon on the table. "Two more sundaes and no skimping on the whipped cream!" The waiter nodded and walked off to start dipping.

"Hey," Robin protested, "hold on. I can't eat another sundae. I'm stuffed."

"Who said it was for you? I'm eating both of them." With a teasing smile Annette sat back in her chair and folded her arms. "Now, start reading."

Over the next few weeks Robin found four more articles about the Supermarket gig. *New York Rocker* ran a long article on the concert and an interview with Reg. *Rolling Stone* included a photo of the band in its "Random Notes" section.

Not surprisingly Marlene Pillsbury's article in *Teen Trend* was more gossip than news. There were lots of photos and the text commented on Reg's good looks and the girls' clothes and hairstyles. Marlene also made a big deal out of Reg and C.C.'s relationship. "We're sure to hear more from these talented young girls in the future," the article concluded. "And who knows, maybe C.C. Collins and Reg Barthwaite are headed down the road to success—with a short stopover at the chapel of love!"

But where was *Rock Rag?* Robin couldn't find it on the newsstand near her house, and none of the bookstores seemed to carry it. Finally she came upon a few copies in a used-record store in the East Village. Eagerly she grabbed a copy and leafed through the pages until she saw the headline OVERNIGHT SENSATION—A SENSATIONAL DEBUT! Holding her breath, she skimmed over the article, searching for her name.

There it was! "Robin Quinn's songs have an energy and passion reminiscent of bands like U2 and Big Country," she read, blushing with pleasure. "Her lyrics are sometimes too obvious and her melodies are weak"—Oh, yeah? Robin thought indignantly. A lot *he* knows!—"but the one thing never in doubt is her sincerity. Furthermore, her guitar playing is technically competent and surprisingly original. If she keeps improving, there's no doubt in my mind that Robin Quinn will someday be a star."

At home Robin cut out Ian's article and taped it to the wall next to her bed. Each night before she turned out the light, she gazed up at the headline and thought about the things Ian had written about her. Sometimes she fell asleep whispering the article's last line: "There's no doubt in my mind that Robin Quinn will someday be a star."

Unfortunately that someday looked as if it was still a long way away. During the weeks after the Supermarket gig Robin received phone calls from three personal managers and two record companies. In each case the person calling had been at the concert or had read about it in the paper and wanted to know what Overnight Sensation was doing now. Were they performing around town? Making a demo tape? Looking for a record deal?

Reluctantly Robin told the truth. The band had broken up. They were hoping to get back together soon, but . . .

No one wanted to hear any more. It was the band they were interested in. Not C.C.'s singing or Robin's songs or any other single aspect of the group, but the group itself. That special combination known as Overnight Sensation. Nothing else would do.

The rest of December passed slowly. Robin tried calling Gail a few more times, but she was never allowed to come to the phone. Meanwhile Annette and Robin were getting together to talk and listen to records. Every week they promised themselves they were going to put together a new band. Maybe they'd find two new girls. Or two boys. Maybe a saxophone player or another guitarist. But deep inside, both of them knew it was all just talk. The only people they really wanted to play with were Gail and C.C. But how?

Now that she had some time on her hands, Robin turned her attention to school and her upcoming exams. She'd spent all semester thinking about the band, and her grades showed it. Even if she aced her finals, she realized, she'd be lucky if she ended up with all C's.

Annette had the same problem. Her grades had never been much above average, but now she was in danger of failing. Plus, there was the question of college. She hadn't applied anywhere yet and she wasn't sure she wanted to. But if not college, what then? Technical school? A job? Annette had no idea. All she knew for sure was that, come June, she was moving out of her parents' house and finding a place of her own.

Time dragged on, and eventually the girls realized that Christmas was only a week away. But even the thought of school vacation and presents couldn't cheer up Annette and Robin. Without Overnight Sensation even Christmas was a bore.

‖‖‖‖‖‖‖‖‖‖‖‖‖‖‖‖‖‖‖‖ **18**

It was New Year's Eve and C.C. was trudging down West Broadway on her way to Reg's loft. The wind blew the falling snow in her eyes, but she just lowered her head and kept shuffling along. Pulling a bottle of brandy from her coat pocket, she stopped to take a sip. As the brown liquid slid down her throat, she thought about the time she'd sat with the girls in the auditorium of Annette's high school, drinking brandy and talking about love.

"I guess I'm going to have to choose," Robin had said. "Love or music. You can't have both."

"You can have both, if you want," C.C. had confidently told them. "You just have to look for them in the same place."

C.C. put the bottle back in her pocket and laughed ruefully. A lot *I* knew, she told herself. Turning down Greene Street, she stopped in front of the warehouse and sat down on the snow-covered steps. From upstairs she could hear the faint sounds of Reg's New Year's Eve party—music, the buzz of conversation, a peal of high-pitched laughter.

C.C. took a cigarette from her purse and lit up. By now Reg was undoubtedly wondering where she was. After all, the new band was going to perform at midnight and it was already after eleven o'clock.

The world debut of The C.C. Collins Band. C.C. sighed. This was her big night and she knew she should be happy. But how could she be? Ever since the Supermarket gig practically nothing had turned out the way she'd expected.

For starters Reg had blamed her for what happened that

night. "I counted on you to make sure those girls signed the contracts," he'd said angrily as they drove to the publicity party in his beat-up white MG. "You told me everything was set. What happened?"

"I don't know," C.C. had answered earnestly. "I had no idea Robin was going to take over the show. I was as surprised as you were."

"Don't give me that. You must have known something was going on. Why didn't you tell me the band was getting together without me to play Robin's songs?"

"I'm sorry," she moaned. "I didn't think it was important. We were just fooling around."

"Just fooling around? I wouldn't call what happened tonight fooling around. You girls made me look like an idiot. And after all I've done for you!"

C.C. tried to smile. "Don't worry, Reg," she told him, reaching out to touch his hand. "Our new band will be even better than C.C. and the Seniors. You said so yourself."

Reg pulled his hand away and eyed her with disgust. "Well, I had to say something, didn't I? I just hope I can make a few bucks off you so this whole thing won't be a total loss."

After that Reg had stopped asking C.C. up to his apartment. When she called him, he said he was too busy to talk. The one time she showed up unannounced, he refused to let her in. "From now on," he said coldly, "I think we should keep our relationship strictly business."

Meanwhile Reg put together a backup band and started rehearsing. The four guys who played behind C.C. were all in their thirties—seasoned studio musicians who made it clear they regarded the band as nothing more than a job. During rehearsals they concentrated on the music and rarely spoke. When the rehearsal was over, they hurried off to meet their girlfriends or pick up their kids or play at studio sessions across town.

The music Reg selected for the band was just this side of heavy metal. "No more pop songs," he told her, "and no more innocence. This band is going to make people forget that C.C.

and the Seniors ever existed. You're going to be wild, dangerous, and sexy as hell."

Consequently C.C. was expected to belt out each song with
the intensity of Pat Benatar while slinking across the stage like
a street-wise Marilyn Monroe. After the first two weeks she
developed laryngitis. Reg was furious and C.C. took to drinking
more and more brandy during every rehearsal. It helped her
voice, but it also made her high, and when she felt like that, she
made so many mistakes that Reg yelled at her anyway.

Through it all C.C. found herself thinking more and more
about Kurt. She hadn't seen him since their encounter in the
men's room, and in a way, she was glad. After all, the whole
thing was so embarrassing! Even so, she wished desperately that
he would call her. She longed to look into his thoughtful brown
eyes and hear his soft, sweet voice. She wanted to feel his arms
around her and kiss his lips—not just a friendly little kiss for
luck, but a real one—deep and warm and tender.

When Mrs. Collins had sat down with C.C. to decide whom
they would invite to be her escorts at the coming-out party,
C.C. had immediately suggested Kurt. Mrs. Collins was delighted and quickly added him to the list. A week later Kurt
sent back his RSVP. He was coming!

C.C. was excited, but she was scared too. She had no idea
how Kurt felt about her, and the more she thought about it, the
more certain she was that he had only accepted her invitation to
be polite. After all, the only date they'd ever had—Patty
Hawthorne's birthday party—had ended with her telling him
she didn't want to see him again, and the only other time they'd
talked to each other she'd been crouching on a sink. Great, C.C.
thought miserably. He probably thinks I'm some kind of nut.

The honk of a car horn brought C.C. back to the present.
Show time, she thought wearily, walking up the stairs and ringing the bell to Reg's loft. Someone buzzed her in and she
trudged upstairs, blowing on her frozen fingers to warm them
up.

Reg was waiting on the landing. "Where the hell have you
been?" he demanded, walking toward her.

C.C. looked into Reg's steel-blue eyes. There was something about him that still excited her. She knew it was crazy to care about him, but she couldn't help it. She wanted him to look at her the way he used to, when his eyes had undressed her and his smile had made it clear he liked what he saw. "I—I'm sorry, Reg," she told him. "I just—"

"Shut up and get in there. All the music people who were at the Supermarket gig are here tonight. They're expecting something hot and you better give it to them."

The room was jammed with people. Dance music blasted out of the PA system and everyone was moving to the beat. A large table filled with food and drinks had been set up near the windows. Most of the food was gone but the liquor was still flowing. C.C. threw her coat on a chair and made her way to the bar. She was wearing clothes Reg had picked out for her—a black leather jump suit, red high heels, and fingerless red leather gloves.

With a glass of brandy in her hand C.C. greeted the backup band and fielded questions from music people and reporters. Despite her makeup and sophisticated clothing C.C. found it hard to feel grown-up tonight. All the party guests seemed to be friends or business associates of Reg, and they all looked at least ten years older than she. C.C. did her best to impress them, but she wished she had Annette and Robin and Gail beside her for moral support.

Marlene Pillsbury was one of the reporters Reg had invited. She quickly cornered C.C. and demanded to know if her romance with Reg was still on. It was all C.C. could do to smile and say coyly, "Why don't you ask him?"

"I hear your old band is out of business," Marlene said with a wink. "I guess you certainly showed them."

It was hard enough to lie about Reg, but C.C. found it impossible to hide her feelings about Overnight Sensation. "If you think you're going to get me to say something catty about my old band, forget it," she told Marlene. "Those girls are my friends and I had more fun singing with them than I've ever had before or since."

Marlene raised her eyebrows. "Oh? Can I quote you on that?"

"Write whatever you want," C.C. retorted. "Just leave me alone."

C.C. turned away just as Reg walked up. "It's almost midnight," he told her. "Put down that drink and get ready."

The band was already tuning up. C.C. gulped down the rest of her drink and hurried to join them. Stepping up behind the mike stand she surveyed her audience. Most of the people at the party were pretty high by now, either from liquor or from the grass she'd noticed some people smoking.

Reg joined C.C. behind the microphone. "It's midnight!" he yelled, throwing his arm around her waist. "Happy New Year!" The crowd let out a drunken cheer. "And now, rock 'n' roll's next superstars—The C.C. Collins Band!"

Reg joined the crowd and the band broke into "Machine Gun Mama." C.C. went into her act, just the way Reg had taught her. She stood with her legs apart and one hip thrust forward. With a sneer on her face she began to sing.

"Baby, baby, don't you mess with me,
I'm a tough little mama and I do as I please.
I got a machine gun where most girls have a heart,
And if you do me wrong I'm gonna blast you apart!"

The crowd was definitely up. They danced and drank and clapped along. When the song was over, they cheered wildly. C.C. spotted Reg leaning against the wall near the door. He looked pleased.

C.C. turned her back on the audience and sighed. I should be happy, she told herself. The band is really hot tonight, and my voice is holding up just fine.

But no matter how good she sounded, it just wasn't the same as when she sang with Overnight Sensation. When the girls tore into "You Can't Stop Me Now," she got excited and her excitement came across in everything she did. She danced and swayed, feeding off the energy of Robin's guitar lines, Gail's steady bass, and Annette's pounding bass drum.

But when the new band played "Machine Gun Mama," C.C. just felt bored. The music meant nothing to her, and the lyrics were just plain silly. Even knowing that she was the center of attention didn't move her. It pleased her, of course, but singing to a bunch of stoned thirty-year-olds just wasn't the same as being on stage at the Supermarket with all those teenagers yelling out the chorus of "Free to Be." Now, *that* was exciting!

The concert dragged on. C.C. sang ten more songs, including "Rev My Motor," "Bad Girl," and "Heartbreak on Highway 109." Through it all the crowd danced, drank, smoked, and cheered with wild abandon.

C.C. was singing the finale—"Rock 'n' Roll Shoot Out"— when she noticed Reg standing near the bar with Marlene Pillsbury. As she watched, he slipped his arms around Marlene's waist and kissed her passionately.

C.C. felt a pain in her heart as real as if she'd been shot. The song ended and the crowd roared its approval, but she turned away without acknowledging their applause. All she wanted was to get out of there, to escape. She couldn't face any reporters now. And most of all she couldn't face Reg. Hoping no one would notice the tears in her eyes she lowered her head and pushed her way toward the door.

But before she could take more than a few steps Reg was at her side, smiling as if he hadn't a care in the world. "Not bad," he said under his breath. "Your voice gave out on the last song, though."

"Reg—" C.C. began, her voice trembling.

But Reg wasn't listening. The crowd was closing in, and he said loudly, "This young lady deserves a drink. Come on over to the bar, everybody."

Too miserable to resist, C.C. let Reg lead her over to the bar and hand her a drink. Reporters and music people clustered around her, asking questions, making jokes, complimenting her on her performance. Reg stood beside her, smiling his usual insincere smile. What a fake! she thought as she watched him. His arm rested heavily on her shoulder, weighing her down. She tried to pull away, but he held her tight.

"What happened to Overnight Sensation?" someone asked. "Are they still together?"

"Who knows?" Reg replied casually. "They're yesterday's news." He squeezed C.C.'s shoulder. "The new year belongs to the C.C. Collins Band!"

"I'll drink to that!" someone shouted. Everybody lifted their glasses.

C.C. gulped down her drink, hoping it would dull her senses and make her forget. But her mind refused to slow down. In fact, for the first time in months, everything seemed perfectly clear.

What a fool I've been, C.C. thought bitterly. For the last four months I've done everything Reg told me to do. When he told me to sign the contract, I signed. When he wanted to sleep with me, I gave in without a murmur. Whatever he told me to sing, I sang. When he told me to wear a cheerleader outfit and sing pop songs, I didn't protest. When he wanted me to wear black leather and sing "Machine Gun Mama," I said sure.

All that, just because I wanted to be a rock star! And what have I got to show for it? I'm singing songs I don't like with people I don't like while Reg treats me like dirt.

Suddenly Reg pulled his arm off C.C.'s shoulder. "I'll be back in a minute," he muttered, hurrying off into the crowd.

C.C. stood on her toes and tried to see where Reg was headed. He seemed to be moving toward the door, and a second later she understood why. Marlene Pillsbury was putting on her coat and hat, preparing to leave. Reg caught up with her just as she was walking out the door. He grabbed her and pulled her close, then leaned over to whisper in her ear.

C.C. felt like screaming. What am I doing here? she asked herself. Why am I putting up with all this? She waited for an answer, but the only reason she could think of was the contract, that stupid piece of paper she'd signed because Reg had told her to. If it weren't for that, she'd have walked out on Reg when the other girls did. If it weren't for that, Overnight Sensation would still exist.

"Excuse me, C.C., there's a rumor going around that Reg is

going to hire the girls from your old band to be backup singers with the C.C. Collins Band." C.C. looked up to find an eager reporter thrusting a tape recorder at her face. "Is there any truth to that rumor?" he asked.

"Oh, for God's sake!" C.C. cried, pushing the tape recorder away. "Why doesn't everybody just leave me alone!" Frantically she threw down her glass and pushed her way through the crowd. People turned to stare at her, but she just grabbed her coat and rushed out the door.

Reg and Marlene were on the landing, passionately embracing. When C.C. burst through the door, they gasped and jumped apart. Quickly regaining his composure Reg ran a hand through his hair and smiled. "Hello, C.C.," he said smoothly.

"Get out of my way," C.C. cried. "I can't stay in this band another minute. I quit!"

Reg laughed. "You can't do that."

"Why? Because I signed a contract? Well, I don't care. I'd rather go to *jail* than spend another minute with you. Now, get out of my way."

Marlene just stood there, caught between embarrassment at being discovered with Reg, and delight at being in on some juicy gossip. Ignoring her, Reg stepped forward and took C.C.'s hands in his. "Come on, C.C.," he said under his breath, "don't be mad. I was just playing up to Marlene so she'd give the band a good write-up. You're the only girl I really care about. You know that, don't you?"

C.C. looked up into Reg's eyes. Even now they had the power to charm her.

"Let's go back to my apartment." Reg laughed softly. "Come on, C.C. You know you love it."

Reg's words brought C.C. down to earth with a bump. The truth was, getting drunk and rolling around with Reg on his couch was definitely not her idea of a good time. *Love* it? C.C. felt like laughing. She didn't even *like* it. "The only time you're nice to me is when you want something," she said bitterly, pulling her hands away. "You don't care about me. You've just been using me, that's all."

"We use each other, C.C.," he said soothingly. "You want to be a rock star, and I want to make some money. There's nothing wrong with that, is there?"

C.C. laughed contemptuously. "If this is what being a rock star is all about, you can have it. I'm going back to Overnight Sensation." She looked at Marlene. "And you can quote me on that." Without another word she turned and started down the stairs.

Reg hung over the landing. "This is your last chance," he called after her. "I'm warning you, C.C. If you leave now, I'm taking you to court."

C.C. looked up into Reg's angry face and smiled. "Good-bye, Reg. And good riddance!"

Out on the street the snow had stopped and the wind was dying down. C.C. turned up her collar and started running down the middle of the street. She wasn't angry anymore—just confused and a little sad. But at the same time, she felt relieved. At last she was free of Reg! It was like having a heavy weight taken off her shoulders. She ran faster and turned onto Canal Street. At the first pay phone she stopped and dialed Annette's house.

The phone rang ten times. Finally a female voice, groggy with sleep, said, "Hello?"

"Hello!" C.C. cried breathlessly. "Mrs. Giraldi? Sorry to call so late, but I have to talk to Annette. It's important!"

"Oh, dear. Well, hold on. I'll see if I can wake her."

C.C. stamped her feet on the pavement and waited impatiently. A minute later Annette came on. "Hello? C.C.? Where are you? Are you all right?"

"I think so," C.C. answered. "In fact, I know I am. I just told Reg what he can do with his stupid contract."

"You what?" Annette asked incredulously.

"I quit! I just walked out. From now on the only band I'm going to sing with is Overnight Sensation." She paused. "Uh, if that's okay with the rest of the group, that is."

"It's okay with me," Annette told her. "You know that. But

Robin may take a little convincing. She doesn't think you rea
care about Overnight Sensation."

"Oh, Annette, I do care. I just got so hung up on Reg and his
stupid promises of fame and fortune that I lost track of what's
really important. But once we get the band back together—"

"But how can we do that?" Annette interrupted. "Even if
you and Robin work everything out, what about Gail? She's
still grounded. I don't think we're ever going to see her again."

"Hmm," C.C. mused, "I'm beginning to get an idea. . . ."

"What do you mean?"

"Just meet me in the city tomorrow. Noon at the Supermarket, okay?"

"Okay!" Annette said eagerly. "See you then."

C.C. hung up the phone and stared up at the star-sprinkled
sky, hoping for inspiration. Having an idea was the easy part.
The trick was going to be figuring out how to turn it into a full-
fledged, honest-to-goodness *plan*.

|||||||||||||||||||||||||| **19**

Gail walked slowly across the Lincoln Center concourse, unbuttoning her coat as she went. It was unusually warm for January—almost fifty degrees—and the New York City sky was
awash with billowy white clouds. With spring in their hearts
businessmen and bag ladies strolled across the plaza or lounged
on the benches, ignoring the dirty snow still melting around the
tree trunks.

Head down, oblivious to the smiling faces around her, Gail
kept walking until she reached the reflecting pool. Standing at
the edge, she looked across the water to the Juilliard School of

The long row of identical square windows seemed to
[l]ack at her, smug and self-satisfied. *We've* got it together,
[se]emed to be saying. What's wrong with you?

[Wit]h a sigh Gail gazed down into the shallow water. In the
[reflecti]on the Juilliard building appeared to be hanging upside
[down o]ver her head. Once the stately white façade had seemed
[a s]hrine to her, a symbol of art and beauty. Now, however,
[the] place seemed more like a prison than a sanctuary. Once she
[e]ntered those doors, she'd be thrown full force into the world of
classical music. Rock 'n' roll would have to left behind.

Just then a gust of wind disturbed the surface of the water
and the whole scene dissolved before her eyes. Blinking, she
glanced at her watch. "Oh, no!" she moaned. She had less than
five minutes to get to her piano lesson. Turning her back on the
Juilliard School, she took off across the concourse, walking fast.

By the time Gail turned onto West End Avenue, her heart
was pounding and she was breathing hard. Stopping in front of
Mr. Dawson's building, she took a deep breath and tried to
calm down. No good. Her body refused to relax, and Gail knew
it wasn't just because she had run the last two blocks. Today she
was going to tell Mr. Dawson about Overnight Sensation.

Stepping up to the door, Gail tried to imagine how Mr. Dawson would react. "I'm open to any kind of music," he'd told
her, "as long as it's challenging and well played." But would
that include rock 'n' roll? Gail had no idea. All she knew was
that her parents respected Mr. Dawson. If he thought it was
okay for Gail to play in a rock band, maybe he could help
persuade her parents to agree. As far as Gail could see, it was
her only hope.

With trembling fingers Gail rang Mr. Dawson's doorbell.
Standing in the elevator, she realized with dismay that she'd
forgotten to bring her music. Oh, well, she thought with a resigned sigh, I didn't practice anyway.

When the elevator opened at the eleventh floor, Gail stepped
out and saw Mr. Dawson standing in the doorway of his apartment. As always the sight of him made her heart quicken. In
her wilder moments she dreamed that Mr. Dawson loved her as

much as she loved him. One day he would take her in his arms and run his long dark fingers over her cheek. "Marry me," he'd whisper, his lips only inches from hers. After that the fantasy was less clear. Vaguely Gail imagined them spending their days inside Mr. Dawson's cool, quiet apartment, playing piano duets and drinking herbal tea. Occasionally they would kiss.

"Gail, you're late!"

Mr. Dawson's stern voice brought Gail back to reality. "I'm sorry," she muttered, hurrying past him into the living room. "I just—"

"No excuses. Just sit down and run through your scales."

Gail cleared her throat and looked up at Mr. Dawson. When their eyes met, her knees felt weak. "Mr. Dawson," she said nervously, "I—I have to talk to you."

Mr. Dawson studied Gail's face, then frowned and nodded. "Sit down," he said, motioning toward the plush flowered sofa. Gail did as she was told and Mr. Dawson lowered himself into a brown butterfly chair. Stretching out his long legs, he looked at Gail across the coffee table. "Now, what is it?" he asked.

Gail sat stiffly on the edge of the sofa and struggled out of her winter coat. "Mr. Dawson," she began hesitantly, "I want to apologize. I know it was wrong of me to tell my parents that you'd asked me to join your chamber-music group. I just needed an excuse to get out of the house and—"

Mr. Dawson shook his head. "Never mind. It's over and done with. Any punishment you deserved was undoubtedly handed out by your parents."

Gail nodded. "They grounded me."

Mr. Dawson chuckled. "Then you paid your dues. Let's forget it." He started to stand up.

"Mr. Dawson, please wait. I have to ask you something. Did my father tell you why I was sneaking out of the house?"

"No," he answered with a frown. "He started, but I didn't want to hear it. It's none of my business."

"But I want to tell you. I *need* to tell you." Gail leaned forward and, after a moment's fearful hesitation, blurted out, "I joined a rock 'n' roll band."

"A band?" Mr. Dawson's expression conveyed a mixture of surprise, amusement, and disbelief. *"You?"*

"Yes. I started out playing keyboards, but now I play bass too. And, Mr. Dawson, I love it!" She was talking fast now, getting it all out. "But my parents made me quit. They want me to be a classical musician, and up until last September I did too. But now, well, I don't know what I want. I love classical music, but when I play with the band, I forget everything except rock 'n' roll."

Suddenly aware she was babbling, Gail stopped and looked sheepishly at Mr. Dawson. He was frowning and the smile was gone from his lips. "Why are you telling me all this?" he asked.

Gail felt sick. Mr. Dawson *did* disapprove. Hanging her head she muttered, "I thought you might understand. I thought if you talked to my parents . . ." Her voice trailed off and she started to stand up. "Never mind. I'm sorry."

"Sit down, Gail." Mr. Dawson's voice was firm and she did as she was told. For a moment no one spoke. Gail looked down at the floor and bit her thumbnail, waiting for what she was sure would be an angry lecture.

"I took you on as a piano student," Mr. Dawson began, "because I felt you had great potential. It seemed to me that if you had the desire, you could create a place for yourself in the world of classical music." He paused. "But since September your playing has been little more than mediocre. Now I understand why." He looked at Gail. "Classical music requires complete devotion. There is absolutely no way you can succeed unless you commit yourself to it completely."

"I—I know," muttered Gail.

"That's why I think you should give this rock group thing a shot."

"What?" Gail gasped, looking up. "You mean you think I should stay in the band?"

"Absolutely. If you try to forget the band and return to your classical training now, you'll only be frustrated. Instead of concentrating on the music you'll be thinking, 'Maybe I would have been happier playing rock 'n' roll.' " He smiled. "What I suggest is this: Let's stop your piano lessons for a while. Just put all your energy into your rock band and see how it goes. If you decide it's not for you, you can always come back."

"But what about my Juilliard audition?" Gail asked, suddenly frightened. "I have to practice for that."

Mr. Dawson folded his arms across his chest. "Gail, you don't *have* to do anything. It's your life and your decision."

"But my parents . . ." Gail said helplessly.

"I'll talk to them. I doubt they're going to like what I have to say, but at least I'll give it a try."

"Oh, Mr. Dawson, this is wonderful! Thank you so much!"

"Forget it," he replied with a flick of his hand. "I understand what you're going through. I've been there myself."

"You have?" she asked incredulously.

Mr. Dawson nodded. "When I was twenty, I discovered jazz. Dizzy Gillespie, Jimmy Smith, Cannonball Adderley . . . those guys just blew me away. I loved it so much I dropped out of college, started a trio, and went on the road. But after a year I'd had enough. Jazz is fine, but my first love is classical music. I went back to school and got my degree."

Gail didn't answer. Right now nothing seemed more exciting than playing rock 'n' roll with Overnight Sensation, but she wondered, was it just a passing phase? Like Mr. Dawson, would she someday want to return to the world of classical music? Well, as Mr. Dawson said, the only way to find out was to try.

Mr. Dawson stood up and motioned toward the piano. "To tell you the truth I don't think much of rock music. It seems too obvious, and much too loud." He chuckled. "But I'm open to anything. Play me something you like and maybe you can turn me into a rock 'n' roll fan."

Nervously Gail walked across the room and sat down at the piano. Mr. Dawson stood facing her, his hands on his hips. Swallowing hard, Gail tried to think of something to play. Suddenly Mr. Dawson's opinion of rock music seemed only too true. Every song Gail could think of seemed hopelessly simple and obvious. Besides, most rock songs needed a band—or at least a singer—to make them sound good. What could she possibly play that Mr. Dawson would like?

Finally Gail settled on an early Jerry Lee Lewis song, "Breathless." Since Lewis was a piano player, the tune was filled with high-speed piano fills. Gail took a deep breath and started playing. The piano shook as she pounded out the funky bass-line and the bluesy chords filled the room.

It wasn't until she'd finished the first chorus that Gail found the courage to glance up at Mr. Dawson. To her surprise he was smiling and tapping his fingers on the piano. Joyfully Gail closed her eyes, threw back her head, and tore into the second verse.

||||||||||||||||||||||||| **20**

C.C. paced across the living room, nervously fingering her pearl necklace. For at least the tenth time in ten minutes she stopped to check her reflection in the gilded mirror that hung above the wing chairs. She was wearing a strapless white silk taffeta dress with a cinched waist and a full, billowing skirt, and her hair was piled high on her head with a few wispy curls dangling over her ears. "Here I am," she told the mirror. "The blushing debutante." She held her palms together in prayer. "Just don't let my dress fall off, that's all I ask."

C.C. pulled aside the curtains and looked out at the front lawn. Her mother had already left for the country club, where she was helping Mrs. Hawthorne supervise the caterers. In the driveway a limousine hired to take C.C. and her escorts to the ball was purring quietly, with the chauffeur at the wheel. But where were her escorts?

C.C. went back to pacing. A few minutes later the doorbell finally rang. She made a quick dash across the room, then stopped to collect herself. Opening the door with what she hoped was perfect calm, she saw Kurt standing on the doorstep, handsome and poised in his black tuxedo. In a flash C.C.'s calm exterior collapsed. Her heart seemed to leap into her throat and her knees felt wobbly. "Hi, Kurt," she said breathlessly.

He produced a bouquet of orchids from behind his back and grinned. "Good evening, you vision of loveliness, you. Crawled out of any bathroom windows lately?"

C.C. could feel herself blushing. *I was right,* she thought miserably. *He thinks I'm a real loony.* "You wouldn't understand. . . ." she muttered.

"Hey, relax. I was just teasing you. If you ask me, the Hillsbrook Country Club could use a lot more members like you. I mean, finding you in the men's room was the most interesting thing that ever happened to me at that place—except maybe the time I accidentally pushed the tennis pro into the pool." He handed C.C. the bouquet. "Now, come on. Let's trip the light fantastic."

C.C. laughed. *Hey,* she thought with relief, *maybe he* does *like me, at least a little.* "We can't leave yet," she told him. "I have to wait for my other escorts."

"No problem. I bribed them to drive to the country club themselves. They'll meet us there." He smiled. "Let's go, rock star. The limo awaits."

C.C. ran inside, grabbed her cape and her bag, took one more peek in the mirror, and hurried out the door. The chauffeur was already opening the door of the limousine, and with Kurt at her side, she lifted her skirts and stepped in.

"So tell me," he said as they drove away, "how did your concert turn out? Did you make it to the East Village in time?"

C.C. rolled her eyes and sighed wearily. "I got there on time —close enough, anyway—but everything after that was a real mess."

"Oh, no! What happened?" Kurt asked, a look of concern on his handsome face.

C.C. shook her head. "It's a long story. I don't want to bore you."

"Bore me? Are you kidding? C.C., maybe you haven't figured it out yet, but I'm very interested in everything you have to say." He smiled. "Besides, you look so gorgeous, I just want to sit here and stare at you. Go on," he said, sitting back in the seat and folding his hands in his lap. "Talk."

C.C. giggled with pleasure. "Well, okay. You see, the reason I climbed out of the bathroom window . . ." Quickly she told Kurt all about the band's performance at the Supermarket, including the backstage breakup. Kurt had a dozen questions, and before she knew it, she had told him everything about the band from the first rehearsal right through to Reg's New Year's Eve party. The only thing she left out was her romantic involvement with Reg. There was no way she was going to tell Kurt about *that!*

"So what happens now?" he asked eagerly. "Are you going to start Overnight Sensation up again?"

"I hope so. It's not that easy, though. First I have to make sure the girls really want me back." She shook her head. "I have a plan, but who knows if it's going to work."

"I'm not worried," Kurt said with a wry smile. "You seem like a girl who isn't afraid to go after what she wants—even if it means crawling out of every bathroom window in Manhattan."

C.C. laughed with pleasure. Suddenly Kurt leaned over and kissed her softly on the cheek. The touch of his lips left her breathless with joy. She tried to speak, but before she could get any words out, the limousine pulled up in front of the country club and the chauffeur jumped out and opened the door. Kurt stepped out and offered his arm.

Walking up the steps to the country club, C.C. felt her stomach filling with butterflies. Up until this moment she'd been too wrapped up in Kurt to think about anything else, but now it all came back to her. Her father had promised to come tonight. He was probably inside right now. For the first time in—how long had it been?—five months, she was going to see him again!

But what if he didn't show up? The thought made her want

to cry. She could still hear her mother saying, "Of course your father will be there. He said he would." But C.C. wasn't convinced. After all, she reminded herself, this wouldn't be the first time he'd promised to see me and then not shown up.

Kurt glanced at C.C. as they walked into the lobby. "Is something wrong?" he asked with a concerned frown. "You look upset."

"It's my father," she admitted. "He's supposed to be here tonight. I haven't seen him since he moved out. He said he'd come, but . . ."

Kurt took C.C.'s hand and squeezed it. "He'll be here," he said softly, and just the sound of his voice made her feel better. With her head held high she walked with Kurt into the ballroom. All the debs and some of their escorts were there, along with most of the mothers and fathers. None of the other guests had arrived yet.

C.C. stopped at the door and scanned the crowd, searching for her father. "Just be here, Daddy," she whispered to herself. *"Please."*

Then suddenly she spotted him. He was over by the bandstand, talking with her mother. In his black tuxedo he looked handsome and distinguished, and C.C.'s heart swelled with love. Grabbing Kurt's hand, she hurried down the stairs and across the ballroom.

"Daddy!" she cried as she came up beside him.

Mr. Collins looked up. For a moment he just stood there, staring at his daughter as if he'd never seen her before. C.C.'s heart stood still. She longed to rush into her father's arms, but she felt shy and awkward. Oh, God, she thought miserably, why doesn't he say something?

Then, slowly, Mr. Collins's face broke into a radiant smile. "Cathy!" he exclaimed, holding out his arms. "My little girl!"

C.C. rushed into his outstretched arms and rested her head on his shoulder. She felt wonderful—warm and protected and loved—and in her heart she forgave her father for everything.

Finally Mr. Collins pulled back and put his hands on C.C.'s

shoulders. "I hardly recognized you," he told her. "You look so grown up!"

That was exactly what C.C. wanted to hear. Happily, she held out her arms and spun around, showing off her dress. "Do you like it?" she asked.

Her father smiled warmly. "You look lovely. Just lovely."

Mrs. Collins had tactfully drawn Kurt aside and was chatting away in her usual breezy manner. Her eyes, however, were constantly darting to the side, taking in her husband's every move. Now she stepped up beside Mr. Collins and slipped her arm through his. "Well, here we are," she said cheerfully. "The whole family together again."

Mr. Collins smiled uncomfortably. "This is C.C.'s big night," he said, carefully avoiding any references to family unity.

I know what she's thinking, C.C. thought, eyeing her mother critically. She sees tonight as her big chance to win him back. C.C. frowned and looked away. Her mother's tactics were so obvious—a low-cut evening gown, a coy smile, a few not-so-subtle comments about "the whole family together again." It was pitiful. Still, deep down, C.C. couldn't help wishing her mother would succeed. Maybe she's right, she told herself. Daddy's just going through a midlife crisis. Pretty soon he'll get tired of running around and decide to come back home. Maybe even tonight.

Before the conversation could continue, Mitzi Searles's mother sidled up to Mrs. Collins and whispered, "We're having a small problem with the caterer. It's about the champagne. . . ."

Mr. Collins waited until his wife had left and Kurt had been drawn into conversation with some other boys. "I want to talk to you, Catherine," he said sternly. "Your mother tells me you've been quite a handful lately. She says that last month you ran off in the middle of a meeting for the debs and their mothers."

C.C. swallowed hard. She'd been wondering if her mother had told him what had been going on the last few months. Now she knew. "I had to, Daddy. My rock group was performing at the Supermarket that night. I couldn't be late for that."

"Hmm. C.C., I don't approve of this at all. You've been brought up with all the advantages. You can do anything you want with your life. Why do you have to waste your time singing in a rock 'n' roll band?"

"It's not a waste," C.C. answered impetuously. "Besides, what right have you got to tell me what I can or can't do? You haven't even been to see me since you moved out."

Mr. Collins stared down at his daughter. C.C. was sure he was about to explode, but before he could say anything Mrs. Hawthorne appeared at their side. "It's time to set up the receiving line," she said in a loud whisper. "Places, please. Places."

The girls lined up with their mothers at the entrance of the ballroom. Since C.C. had sneaked out of the debs' rehearsal the day of the Supermarket gig, she wasn't sure what she was supposed to do. Crossing her white-gloved fingers behind her back she took her place and hoped for the best.

The first guests were arriving now and Mrs. Collins was all smiles. "Good evening, Tom," she said as the first group of people moved through the line. "I'd like you to meet my daughter, Catherine. Catherine, this is Mr. Scridlow. Mr. Scridlow is on the board of directors here at the country club."

"Good evening, Mr. Scridlow." C.C. shook hands and curtsied, hoping that was what she was supposed to do. There was no time to worry about it, though, because at least a dozen other people were lining up, awaiting their turn to meet the girls. Fixing a pleasant smile on her face, C.C. turned to shake hands with the next one.

During the introductions the ten members of the Stanley Winkleman Dance Band were discreetly taking their places on the bandstand. When most of the guests had been through the line, Stanley Winkleman tapped his baton on a music stand and the band began to play. As the receiving line broke up, Mr. Collins walked up to C.C. "Shall we dance?" he asked, his face unsmiling.

Afraid to meet her father's eyes C.C. nodded and stepped into his arms. "You know, you're right, Cathy," he said softly.

Surprised, C.C. looked at him. "About what?" she asked.

"About what you said a few minutes ago. I have no right to tell you how to run your life. I don't live with you and your mother anymore. And I haven't been to see you since I moved out."

C.C. didn't know what to say. "Well . . ." she muttered.

"This has been a difficult time for me, Catherine," Mr. Collins continued. "I wanted to see you, but I just didn't know what to say to you. How could I tell you my plans when I didn't know them myself?"

They danced on in silence for a minute. Mr. Collins stared pensively at the floor. Then, clearing his throat, he said, "I've been rethinking my whole life, trying to understand where I've been and where I want to go. It was Bonnie who really got me pointed in the right direction, I guess. . . ."

"Who's Bonnie?" C.C. asked.

Mr. Collins laughed uncomfortably. "Oh, I'm sorry. I forgot you don't know her name. Bonnie is the woman I've been seeing."

"You mean that lady from Connecticut?"

"That's right. Thanks to her I've finally been able to make some very important decisions."

C.C. took a deep breath and looked into her father's eyes. She wished with all her heart that he was going to say he'd decided to come back to his wife and daughter. But she knew he wasn't.

"I'm divorcing your mother," Mr. Collins said simply.

C.C. nodded. Now that her father had actually said it, she didn't feel much of anything. Her mind was a blank and her body was numb.

"But, Cathy," Mr. Collins added quickly, "I want you to know I'm going to make this up to you. Anything you want, just name it. Nothing's too good for my little girl."

C.C. knew what *that* meant. Just like the diamond necklace he sent me for my graduation, she told herself. Instead of spending any time with me, he's going to dole out some more consolation prizes. C.C. sighed. Well, I was going to ask for his help anyway. I might as well do it now. "Daddy, I have a favor to ask."

"Anything," Mr. Collins replied.

"It's about the rock band. You see, the guy who started the group wanted us to sign a contract giving him the right to manage us, and, well . . . I signed it."

Mr. Collins stopped dancing. "Go on."

"Well, you see, the other girls didn't sign. And now we don't want this guy to be our manager, but he says I have to do what he wants because I signed the contract." She looked up at her father. "Do I have to, Daddy?"

Mr. Collins frowned. "Catherine, you should know better than to sign something without consulting your mother or me. I'm very disappointed in you."

"I'm sorry. I see now what a big mistake I made, but—"

"Wait a minute!" Mr. Collins looked closely at C.C. "When's your birthday?"

"The end of this month," C.C. replied, wondering what her father was getting at. "January thirtieth."

Mr. Collins laughed loudly. "Catherine," he said, "you're only seventeen. That contract isn't valid."

C.C. stared at her father in disbelief. "It's not? But Reg said—"

"I don't care what anybody said. Until you're eighteen, everything you sign has to be approved by your parents. That contract is meaningless." He smiled reassuringly. "I'll call my lawyer on Monday and have him send a letter to this so-called manager of yours. That should take care of everything."

C.C. could hardly believe her ears. She thought back to the day she auditioned for the band. Reg had asked her how old she was and to make him think she was more grown up, she'd told him she was eighteen. C.C. smiled. The joke's on you, Reg, she thought with delight.

"Thanks, Daddy," C.C. said gratefully. "And just one more thing. I never told Mother about signing the contract. Do you think we could keep it a secret just between us two?"

Mr. Collins looked at C.C. "On one condition. Promise me you won't say anything to your mother about the divorce. I haven't told her yet and I don't want to get into a fight about it this evening. I'll talk to her about everything tomorrow."

"Okay," C.C. agreed.

Mr. Collins smiled. "That's my girl."

The song ended and everyone applauded politely. C.C. looked up to find Kurt standing at her side. "May I have this dance?" he asked suavely.

Mr. Collins patted C.C.'s shoulder, then turned and walked off the dance floor. The band swung into a plodding version of the Billy Joel song "Just the Way You Are" and Kurt held out his hands. Stepping into his arms, C.C. let him lead her around the room.

"The other guys are dying to dance with you," he told her. "But I threatened to beat them up if they didn't let me go first." He chuckled. "I don't think they were too frightened, but they gave in anyway, maybe out of pity."

C.C. smiled up at him. "Thanks."

"Hey, are you okay?" he asked, looking at her closely. "How did things go with your dad?"

C.C. sighed. "He's divorcing my mother. It wasn't a surprise, really, but . . . well, it's still tough to take."

Kurt didn't answer. Instead he stopped dancing and held her close. C.C. didn't resist. Gratefully she rested her head against his shoulder and hugged back. The other dancers were glancing at them disapprovingly, but she didn't care. Here in Kurt's arms all the problems of the last few months seemed just to fade away. She felt warm and protected and blissfully happy.

It was never like this with Reg, she suddenly realized. When he was around I was always nervous and worried. *Does he like me? Am I cool enough? If I do everything he tells me, will he make me a star?* C.C. had to laugh. In a way it was no different from the way her parents acted, always struggling to "do the right thing" and "meet the right people." The only difference was that they wanted to be accepted into society and she wanted to be accepted into the rock 'n' roll scene.

Well, I still want to be part of the rock scene, she told herself. That hasn't changed. But from now on I'm going to do it on my own terms, by being myself and singing the music I want to sing. And by hanging around people I really care about. People like Annette and Gail and Robin. And Kurt.

C.C. stepped back and looked at him. "Remember after Patty Hawthorne's party," she said shyly, "when you asked me if I'd go out with you sometime?"

He nodded. "Sure I do. You said you were busy with the band."

"Yeah, well, the band may take up a lot of time, but that doesn't mean I'm too busy to see you. In fact, I can't think of anything I'd like more."

"All *right!*" Grinning, Kurt grabbed her and swept her across the floor as gracefully as if he were Fred Astaire playing a big love scene with Ginger Rogers. "See," he whispered, holding her close and swaying with the music, "I told you all this stuff could be fun. Country clubs, coming-out parties, the whole bit. You just have to be with the right person."

C.C. gazed into Kurt's dark-brown eyes and let out a blissful sigh. "Yeah," she said dreamily. And to herself she added, *Someone exactly like you.*

‖‖‖‖‖‖‖‖‖‖‖‖‖‖‖‖‖ **21**

Robin double-parked her orange Toyota in front of the Supermarket and turned on the emergency flashers. "All right," she said impatiently, turning to Annette, "we're here. Now what?"

"Relax," she replied. "C.C.'ll be here soon." She smiled mysteriously. "We've got a couple of surprises in store for you and Gail."

"C.C.? Gail? What are you talking about?" When Annette didn't answer, she threw her head back and let out an exasperated sigh. "Come on, Annette. First you tell me to put my guitar in the car and come pick you up. Then you make me help you load all your drums in the backseat. Now you tell me to drive to the Supermarket. You gotta tell me what's up. I can't stand the suspense!"

Annette laughed. "Cool your jets. You'll find out soon enough." She rolled down her window and leaned out. "Hey, here they come now!"

Robin threw open the door and leaped out. C.C. and Gail were walking down the sidewalk toward her. "Gail!" she cried. "I can't believe it!" Robin ran down the sidewalk with Annette close behind. When Gail saw them coming, she met them halfway and the three friends fell into each other's arms, laughing with delight. "I was beginning to think I'd never see you again," Robin said with amazement. "How did you get out of the house?"

Gail swallowed hard. "It was all C.C.'s doing, really. She called my big brother and talked him into helping us. He told my parents we were going to a Mozart concert at Lincoln Center. I—I wasn't going to lie to them anymore, but I just *had* to see you, and well . . ."

But Robin wasn't listening. She turned to C.C. and regarded her with a mixture of amazement and delight. "Hey, this is great! Thanks!" Suddenly she realized that although she'd hugged Gail as soon as she saw her, she'd barely acknowledged C.C.'s presence. But then why should I? Robin thought defensively. C.C. always cared about Reg more than Overnight Sensation. It's only now when things have fallen apart with him that she comes running back, trying to make friends again.

As if she'd read Robin's mind, C.C. turned to her and said, "I know you're pissed at me, Robin. You think I cared more about Reg than—"

"Overnight Sensation," Robin finished. "Yeah, you're right. I think you're only into rock 'n' roll because it's glamorous. You don't really care about the music. You just want to get famous so you can be seen with a bunch of rock stars."

"You're right," C.C. admitted, "but only partly. I do love the glamor and the excitement of rock. And I do want to be famous. But not if that means taking orders from people like Reg. I was taken in by him for a long time, but finally I realized he was only using me."

"It wasn't just you, C.C.," Annette told her. "We all fell for Reg and his big promises." She smiled knowingly. "It's just that you fell a little harder."

"Yeah, well, that's all over now. I told Reg to take a hike." She looked at each of the girls. "I want to be in Overnight Sensation again," she said earnestly. "I always liked playing our own music better than those dumb songs Reg picked out, anyway. I think we sound great together. And if those reviews we got mean anything, a lot of other people think so too."

"That's right," agreed Gail. "We belong together."

Robin shrugged. "After that night at the Supermarket I was pretty pissed at you, I'll admit. But, hey, I never said I didn't want you in the band. No one could sing my songs better than you do."

"But what about the contract?" Gail asked. "You can't get out of that, can you?"

C.C. grinned. "Oh, yes, I can. My father told me the contract's no good."

"No good?" Robin repeated incredulously. "But how can that be?"

"Well," she said sheepishly, "remember how I told all of you I'm eighteen?"

"Yeah? So?"

"Well, I sort of stretched the truth a little. Actually, I'll be eighteen at the end of this month."

"But—"

"Just listen," C.C. said impatiently. "My father says if you're under eighteen you can't sign a contract without your parents' permission." The girls stared at her blankly. "Don't you get it?" she cried. "The contract doesn't count. It's no good!"

"All *right!*" Robin excláimed. "Now all we have to do is figure out a way to get Gail back in the—"

"Wait a minute, Robin," Gail broke in. *"I* have an announcement to make too." She took a deep breath. "I told my piano teacher about the band and asked him to help me. He's going to talk to my parents and try to convince them to let me rejoin the group. I don't know if they'll listen, but—"

"Way to go, Gail!" Annette shouted ecstatically, slapping her a high five.

"So what are we standing around here for?" Robin asked. "Let's go somewhere and celebrate. My car's right up the street."

"Hold on," C.C. cried, grabbing her arm. "We can't leave now. We've got a concert to play."

Robin stared at her in disbelief. "A concert? What are you talking about?"

"Just what I said." She smiled smugly. "I figured it was up to me to show you guys I'm serious about the band, so I called the owner of the Supermarket and told him we were back together again and looking for work. After all those articles about us in the paper, we're big news, I guess, because he said sure. We're playing a half-hour set tonight before the opening act. Uh, if none of you are too busy, that is. . . ."

Robin let out a shriek and threw her arms around C.C. "I can't believe it! You're incredible! Just amazing!"

C.C. laughed. "I know, I know. Now, come on, troops. We can't keep our fans waiting."

Linking arms, the girls marched down the alley and pounded on the back door of the Supermarket. A moment later it was opened by a lanky young man in jeans and a black-and-white plaid shirt. When Robin saw who it was her heart kicked into overdrive. "I-Ian Harkin!" she stammered. "What are *you* doing here?"

Ian pretended to look hurt. "Well, I can leave if you want.

But then I'd have to take back the bass guitar and all the other equipment I brought for you to use."

"We needed instruments," C.C. explained, "and Annette told me about meeting Ian after the last Supermarket gig. I figured maybe he could help."

"You have his business card on your bureau," Annette added. "Last time I was over, I copied it down and called him."

Robin looked thoughtfully at Ian. Hmm, she told herself, maybe he's not such a bad guy, after all. "Thanks, Ian," she said grudgingly.

"Don't mention it. Listen, you girls better get moving. You're on in fifteen minutes."

"Fifteen minutes!" cried Robin. "We'll barely be set up by then. What about our sound check?"

"That's a luxury reserved for well-known bands. Clubs don't pay much attention to the opening act." He nodded sagely. "You'll learn."

Robin frowned. Just as I thought, she told herself. Stuck up. "Come on, gang," she told the girls. "Let's get to work."

With Ian's help the girls ran out to the car and lugged Annette's drums and Robin's amp inside. There were no roadies to help them now, and no hair stylist to make sure they looked good. They had to set up all their equipment themselves, with only one bored Supermarket sound engineer to show them how to plug into the club's PA system. "This isn't the way rock stars are supposed to be treated," Robin muttered as she and C.C. dragged an amplifier on stage.

"We're not rock stars anymore," C.C. replied. "Just struggling unknowns." She blew her bangs out of her eyes and grinned. "But you know, I think I kind of like it this way."

Hurrying into the wings, the girls made a halfhearted effort to comb their hair and clean themselves up. "This sure is a far cry from matching cheerleader outfits," Annette remarked, looking down at her ripped jeans and sweat-stained gray sweater.

"Well, at least you'll know the audience is judging you on your music," Ian told them, "instead of your looks."

A guy in a Supermarket T-shirt walked up and looked them over. "I'm the manager here. Toby's the name. You kids the opening act?"

"Yes," Robin told him. "We're Overnight Sensation."

"Well, what are you waiting for? We're behind schedule already. Just get out there and introduce yourselves."

Ian leaned over and gave Robin a quick kiss on the cheek. "Go out there and show 'em what you can do," he told her.

Robin's stomach was fluttering, but she wasn't sure if it was from stage fright or Ian's kiss. Before she could chicken out, she ran onstage and strapped on her guitar. As the other girls took their places, she ran up to the microphone and announced, "This band is called Overnight Sensation. Last time we were on this stage, I said you'd be hearing a lot more from us in the future. Well, the future is *tonight!*" She raised her hand above her head and looked around at the girls. " 'Free to Be.' One, two, three, four—"

When Robin dropped her hand, the band hit the opening chord with the force of a tidal wave. "I gotta be free, free to be!" C.C. sang, grabbing the microphone off the stand and running to the edge of the stage. Robin and Gail stood side by side, pointing their guitars at the audience like rock 'n' roll machine guns. Behind them Annette whacked her snare drum as if she were hitting a grand-slam home-run.

The audience surged forward, bouncing and swaying in time to the pounding beat. There weren't any record executives or rock journalists out there this time, but the girls didn't care. They were playing to the people who mattered, kids like themselves who lived and breathed rock 'n' roll.

"You can't know what you want until you try everything," C.C. wailed, "so come on, pretty baby, let me hear you sing FREE TO BE!" As she sang, she looked down at the sea of faces, searching for Kurt. He was supposed to go out to dinner with the partners from his father's law firm tonight, but he'd promised that if there was any chance he could get away, he would rush right over to the Supermarket to see the band. Damn! thought C.C., he isn't there. She turned away, trying not to mind. It wasn't Kurt's fault, she knew that, but still, she couldn't help feeling disappointed.

When the song ended, the crowd let out a cheer of approval. "Thank you!" Robin shouted. "Here's another original called 'Great Expectations.' One, two, three—"

The band broke into a rolling blues rhythm. C.C. pounded out the chords on the electric piano and sang,

> *"I got big plans, great expectations,*
> *But I need love to help me make it.*
> *I need you when the night gets cold,*
> *I need you when my plans all fold,*
> *I need you when my great expectations fall through."*

As she sang, she glanced into the wings. Ian was there, snapping his fingers and nodding approvingly. A couple of roadies from one of the other bands had gathered behind him. While C.C. watched, someone stepped between them and stood next to Ian. Kurt! Joyfully, C.C. caught his eye and grinned. He grinned back and threw her a kiss. Starry-eyed, she belted out the last chorus:

> *"I need you when my world looks blue,*
> *I need you when I feel confused,*
> *I need you when my great expectations fall through."*

After that the band tore through four other songs—two more by Robin, plus Tom Petty's "American Girl" and Marshall Crenshaw's "Rockin' Around in N.Y.C."

"One more!" Toby called from the wings. "You got time for one more!"

"Okay," Robin told the audience, "this is our last song, and in a way it's the story of Overnight Sensation too. It's called 'You Can't Stop Me Now.'" She looked at the other girls. "Come on, let's rock!"

C.C. ran up beside her and started to sing, "Well, I may be crazy, but I got this dream . . ."

When she got to the chorus, Robin leaned into the microphone and grinned at C.C. "You can't stop me now!" they sang together. Annette yelled, raising her drumsticks in a triumphant salute. Gail closed her eyes and let the music envelop her. "No, baby," she sang, more to herself than to the audience, "you can't stop me now!"

Then suddenly it was over and the crowd cheered as they ran off the stage. "Great show!" Ian exclaimed, patting them on the back like a winning football coach.

Kurt applauded as C.C. walked up to him. "Oh, C.C.!" he moaned, pretending to swoon. "Can I have your autograph?"

C.C. giggled. "I didn't think you'd be here tonight," she said. "How did you manage it?"

"Simple. Seeing you sing is a lot more important to me than eating dinner with a bunch of stuffed-shirt lawyers. And that's what I told my dad."

"You're kidding!" C.C. gasped. "Wasn't he mad?"

"Yeah, but not as much as I thought he'd be. I think he's finally getting the idea I wasn't cut out to be a lawyer."

"What a rebel!" she said, shaking her finger. "I guess we're two of a kind."

"You know it, kid." Pulling her close, Kurt took her face in his hands and kissed her deeply.

Robin turned to Annette and Gail. "Who's that?" she asked, indicating Kurt. "The president of the C.C. Collins Fan Club?"

"I heard that," C.C. replied, pretending to be angry. She put her arm around Kurt's waist. "This extremely attractive young man just happens to be my boyfriend. Kurt Vandenburg, meet the band—Robin, Annette, and Gail."

"Hi!" said Kurt. "You were great!"

"Thanks," Annette said, unable to hide her impatience. "Come on, girls, let's go celebrate!"

"Wait a minute!" Robin moaned. "I just realized something. I left my car double-parked out front. It's probably been towed away by now."

"No, it hasn't," Ian broke in. "The keys were still in the ignition, so after you took your guitar inside, I parked the car around the corner."